THE
CALLING
BIRDS

THE CALLING BIRDS

JIM BARRETT

MARIN
PUBLISHING

The Calling Birds

Published by MARIN PUBLISHING

Laguna Woods, California

Copyright ©2019. JIM BARRETT. All rights reserved.

Library of Congress Control Number: 2019901232
BARRETT, JIM, Author
THE CALLING BIRDS
JIM BARRETT

ISBN: 978-1-7336189-0-8

FIC027100 **FICTION** / Romance / Western

DEDICATION

This book is dedicated to all the Native Americans who suffered and died in the process of relocation to the reservations in Oklahoma and other destinations. Their pain and suffering was pathetic, all in the name of expansion for the white man and his way of life. To all who suffered, I extend my heartfelt, though inadequate, apology and can only hope that time helps heal all sins.

CHAPTER ONE

Washington, D.C.   *Spring 1985*

T he plane braked to a halt on the runway as people began to
gather their assorted belongings around them. The flight
attendant's voice came over the plane's intercom to welcome
the arriving passengers to Washington, D.C., and advised they
should not unbuckle their seat belts until they were at the ramp
area. Ken picked up his briefcase and when the plane stopped,
retrieved his small "carry-on" from the overhead bin. A few
business-type passengers were digging through briefcases to find
their boxy mobile phones to advise whomever that they had
landed and to meet them at designated places within the airport,
or to let people back home know that they had arrived.

Ken was one of the first passengers to debark into the main
concourse, and he found the escalators leading to the reception
area. He noticed a group of people in the reception area eager

to meet passengers coming in from the plane. There were three or four young men dressed in black suits holding signs with various names on placards held chest-high. One of the signs had JUDGE ADAMS in bold print and Ken advanced to meet the holder. Another young man at the chauffeur's side stepped forward with his hand extended and welcomed Ken to Washington, D.C.

"Let me take your case, we have a car waiting to take you to the White House," said the young aide. He introduced himself and the chauffeur as well and mentioned that this was the perfect time to visit D.C., dropping the Washington identification as most residents do.

The aide assisted Ken into the back seat and he took the small seat on the side. The limousine eased gently into the traffic to exit the airport area and soon Ken was seeing what the young aide meant about this being a great time to visit the capital. The cherry trees were in full bloom and the colors were spectacular. The aide and driver made small talk about the sites and presence of history as they made their way through traffic to their destination.

The limousine was cleared to enter the White House driveway and pulled slowly to a stop at the entrance. The military aide who opened the door to greet them was smiling and pleasant. Ken asked him where he was from and he replied proudly, "Same place as you, the great state of Texas." This recognition of a common background made Ken smile. In addition to the young aide's likable personality, Ken knew he had training and capabilities to protect the safety of all who resided in or entered the White House. Not just the aide, but the dozens of other young men and women stationed at the residence as well.

The young aide escorted Ken to the security desk located just inside the White House entrance. He introduced Ken to the receptionist who had a stack of clearance files on her desk. She removed one, opened it and compared the eight-by-ten photograph to Ken's appearance. Satisfied that he was indeed Judge Ken Adams, she stated, "We have to be careful to check out everyone who enters the White House. After all, it is the residence of the President and his family."

Ken noted the presence of two tall, athletic, young secret service agents stationed behind the receptionist and smiled at them, knowing they would be well-armed and trained in providing security for the world's most powerful man, his family and staff. Although not visible, Ken was certain there were additional agents available at a quick moment's notice. The receptionist handed Ken an identification tag with his name and picture on it, with a clip to attach to his breast pocket lapel. "Please return your identity badge when you leave. We will have it available for any future visit to the White House," said the receptionist. Ken was certain he had stepped through additional screening sensors at the entrance as well.

"Please follow me, sir," said the young aide as he escorted Ken to an ornate office and asked if he would care for a refreshment or coffee. Ken replied that he was fine but would welcome a chance to simply relax and spend a few moments alone. The aide said that would be fine.

"The President will request your appearance shortly. I'll be outside and, if you need anything, just let me know," he said as he closed the door. Ken had not realized how much the previous twenty-four hours had stressed his mind and body until he found himself completely and totally alone on the comfortable couch. As his mind drifted to recall the amazing occurrences of the previous day, his eyes noted the objects on the desk: the normal paper clips, pens, calendar, and stacks of paper along with a large reading glass. His mind focused on the magnifying glass and drifted back to a time many years before.

CHAPTER TWO

Hendley, Texas   *Fall 1952*

Twelve-year-old Ken Adams stared intently into the display case of the town's only drug store. His vision was focused on the large magnifying glass centered on the top shelf of the display case. The price tag showing $1.75 was clearly visible. Without realizing the presence of the store's owner, Mr. Pelter, Ken was lost in imagining the discoveries to be revealed with such a fine magnifying glass. He figured he still had ten minutes left on his lunch break from school.

"Now, just what would you do with it?" asked Mr. Pelter.

Ken jumped backward, surprised to see Mr. Pelter, complete with a cigar, bifocals, a hearing aid, thinning hair, jowled cheeks and generally grumpy disposition, staring down at him. Unaccustomed to conversation with adults, especially one who was President of the School Board, Deacon in the First Baptist Church, member of the Chamber of Commerce and owner of Pelter's Drug Store, Ken was speechless. Finally, he regained sufficient composure to stutter that he thought the magnifying glass would be an interesting tool to explore the world of miniature items.

"Like what?" asked Mr. Pelter.

"Like oak leaves and mosquitos and dog fleas and chicken feathers and pond water and all those other things," came tumbling out of Ken in an explosion of enthusiasm. As he looked up, Ken was surprised to see a distant faraway look in Mr. Pelter's eyes. It was as if the man was seeing something in his past, a memory of a boyhood long ago.

He slowly looked down and said, "I think we can do business. How much do you have?"

Ken slowly extended his hand to show him the half dollar he had clenched throughout the conversation. Mr. Pelter said that would do fine for a down payment and Ken could pay off the balance at the rate of 25 cents per week.

At twelve years old and with a limited means of economic endeavor, Ken entered the world of high finance, the first of many such deals yet to come.

Ken was anxious to get home from school. The school bus seemed to be moving in slow motion and each stop dragged on interminably. The driver seemed to move even more slowly than usual at each stop, where he had to disgorge himself from the driver's seat to hold up the red stop sign to make sure the smaller children did not run in front of any passing cars.

Ken fingered the magnifying glass in his pocket as he imagined using it to highlight the outline of fossils forever embedded in rocks at his father's gravel pit. Each year his father negotiated an agreement with the county road commissioner to allow the big dump trucks to haul gravel from his pit to repair damaged dirt roads throughout the county. There were lots of roads that needed lots of gravel, and even at a dollar and a half a load, the sum built up over time represented nice extra income which Ken's family enjoyed. The fact that it was expected that Ken's father would make a substantial contribution to the re-election campaign for the county road commissioner at the next election was just the way things worked – no one thought much about it including Ken, until the year his father's friend did not get re-elected. The gravel contract ended immediately and the new road commissioner promptly awarded it to one of his cronies. It was good while it lasted.

When the dirt loader had worked to load the gravel trucks, it occasionally struck a rock too large to be included with the gravel material. The operator pushed these large rocks into a pile so they could be used for filling in major road failures, which sometimes happened after heavy spring rains caused a bridge or an entire road section to be washed out. On a few occasions, Ken had spotted what appeared to be encapsulated fauna fossils in the rocks. With his new magnifying glass he could more closely examine the outlines and try to see if they really were fossils or not.

At last the bus reached Ken's stop and he bolted from the door with a quick backward wave to signal his sense of freedom. He ran through the house, dumped his books in his room, grabbed a slice of bread from the pantry and pulled the peanut butter from the refrigerator.

"My but we are in a hurry today," observed Ken's mother from her stance in front of the gas cookstove. She was well into preparation of supper as Ken's father expected to have his meal on the table when he arrived home from work. Normally the entire family would gather at the supper table at 5:30 and Ken figured he had about an hour to get to the gravel pit and conduct his inspection. He poured himself a glass of milk to help wash down the sandwich and between bites relayed his exploration plans to his mother.

"Have fun – and I hope you find something interesting," she yelled after him as he darted out the back door.

It was about a quarter of a mile from Ken's house to the gravel pit. He jogged the distance easily in two to three minutes. As he jogged along, he observed the trees on his father's property. A heavy frost had come early that year and the leaves were bright with numerous beautiful colors ranging from light brown to gold to red and many hues in between. The sky was blue and clear although they had recently experienced a couple of heavy thunderstorms earlier in the week. As he neared the gravel pit, he saw two ground squirrels scurry away heading to their dens concealed under a mound of rocks. All in all, a gorgeous afternoon of a beautiful fall day. He was happy that his football practice sessions were scheduled for early mornings prior to the start of the school day. The varsity football team's practice sessions were scheduled for afternoons. Ken's young body was strong and well conditioned from his practice sessions, and in addition, he ran or jogged wherever he was going on a daily basis. The gravel loader was quiet since the gravel hauling was done for the day. He located the pile of rocks at the edge of the pit and began his examination with high spirits. Two or three times he thought he had spotted a fossil imprint but each time the magnifying glass revealed the pattern to be nothing more than just color variations or strata changes in the rocks themselves. He spent twenty minutes going over the pile of rocks with no luck and was beginning to think the afternoon would prove to be a waste of time attempting to use his new tool.

As he neared the edge of the gravel pit, he spotted what appeared to be a sharp, small rock protruding from the soil. He flicked it with the toe of his shoe and as it broke free from the dirt he knew exactly what he had found. A complete, authentic flint arrowhead. He picked it up and rubbed the dirt away all the while marveling at the shape and small fine flakes someone had chipped away to give the piece of stone its shape and sharpness. Some of his friends had shown him pieces of arrowheads they had found but no one he knew had ever found one that was complete and undamaged.

As he walked slowly toward home, still rubbing the arrowhead, he heard a low rumble and felt a tremor from the ground at the same time. At first he thought it might be an approaching thunderstorm but as he turned to look over his shoulder, he got the shock of his life. A herd of buffalo was heading straight for him in a stampede frenzy. He looked to his left and spotted a small earth mound with a sharp ledge about three feet high. He landed on his stomach under the ledge just as the first buffaloes passed over and around him. The thunder of the hooves and snorting of the animals' noses were so loud, Ken threw his hands over his ears to shut out the noise. As he laid close to his protective ledge, he could see nothing but buffalo as they swarmed past him in their uncontrolled run. The dust they kicked up blotted out the sun and made it hard for him to breathe. Ken glimpsed an Indian brave mounted on a horse running alongside the herd, and just as quickly as they appeared, they were gone – swallowed up in the cloud of dust and dirt from the stampeding herd. A horse plunged over the mound, stumbled and spilled his rider directly near the ledge where Ken had taken refuge. The rider quickly scrambled on all fours for the shelter of the mound. Ken found himself staring face-to-face in the wide eyes of a young Indian boy – no more than twelve or thirteen years old. The two of them pressed their bodies as tightly against the earth ledge as they possibly could. Although the number of buffaloes stampeding by seemed to be diminishing, there were still plenty leaping over and around the earth mound. At last, the sound of the herd began to subside and the dust and dirt began to settle. A powerfully built Indian brave on a plunging horse pulled up near the mound and the young brave scampered out and stood erect before the fiercely outfitted warrior. Although he spoke an Indian dialect, Ken could understand their conversation.

"Where is your horse?" asked the warrior.

"He fell down – I hid there," responded the young brave pointing to the spot he and Ken had shared during the stampede.

"It is good you did not die," said the warrior. "Come – the hunt is done – now the People will feast."

With that he reached down his hand and the young brave swung up onto the horse behind the warrior and they were gone in a thunder of hooves.

Ken scrambled to his feet. His legs shook and he folded back down to a kneeling position and simply stared in the direction the Indians had ridden. Ken looked around and was surprised to see absolutely no evidence of what he had just witnessed. No earth marks, no trampled grass – nothing. He stood up and made a slow, complete circle – no evidence in any direction of the buffalo stampede he had just witnessed. Or had he just imagined it all?

CHAPTER THREE

Ken slowly made his way home and arrived just as his father entered the kitchen. His parents touched lightly as his father made his way to the kitchen table which had been prepared for the four of them by his mother. Ken washed his hands in the bathroom and took his seat. His father located his regular TV show – the country western show from Wichita Falls – as Ken and his younger brother, Tommy, began eating their supper. It was pretty much predictable fare – fried chicken, mashed potatoes, gravy, sliced tomatoes, cornbread and the ever-present iced tea. The iced tea was a necessity since Ken's father demanded the standard midwestern culinary style of "If it don't crunch, it ain't done."

Ken waited for a commercial break in the TV show and then asked his father, "Do you think this area ever had buffalo herds?"

"Sure," responded his father between bites, "over the past thousands of years, there could have been many occasions when herds made their way through here. They say before the white man came, some of the herds had many thousands of buffalo. The Indians lived off the buffalo." At this, he returned to his TV program.

Ken continued eating and at the next break announced he had found an arrowhead down near the gravel pit.

"Let me see it – let me see it," piped in his little brother.

Ken carefully extracted the arrowhead from his pocket and held it out for Tommy to see.

"Wow, that's a real arrowhead," said Tommy. "Can I hold it? Can I? Can I?" he yelped.

Ken's father said, "I've heard of people finding old arrowheads around here but the only ones I ever saw had been broken. That's the first complete arrowhead I've seen."

Ken announced, "I'm taking it to school tomorrow to show to Mr. Kennedy. He's always talking about Indians and maybe he can help me learn more about it." Mr. Kennedy was his Junior High School history teacher and Ken was in his state history class this year. He slipped the arrowhead back into his pocket and resumed eating.

Ken's mother said, "You know that arrowhead could be hundreds maybe even thousands of years old – it may have a very great history – if only we could know." Ken looked out the window and was mesmerized envisioning the passing of history right before his eyes. The idea that Indians, buffaloes, horses, wild turkeys – the whole assemblage – had lived, walked, hunted and died right on the very land he had just walked that afternoon was like seeing a movie all in his own imagination.

The next morning, Ken dismounted the school bus as quickly as the door opened and dashed down the school hallway to Mr. Kennedy's room. As usual, the teacher had arrived early and was in the process of arranging his lesson plans for the classes he would teach that day.

"You're in quite a hurry," acknowledged Mr. Kennedy when Ken bolted through the door. Ken didn't say anything – he just held out his hand with the arrowhead openly displayed. Mr. Kennedy took a long, careful look, slowly took the arrowhead from Ken's hand and began a close examination. "Now that's one of the best arrowheads I've ever seen – no breaks – no cracks – a real find. And just where did you get this?" he asked.

"Down by my dad's gravel pit. The point was just sticking out of the ground and I pushed it with my foot and it popped out."

"Very interesting," marveled Mr. Kennedy. "It looks like it could be from the Pawnee tribe. You know they used to roam the plains following the buffalo herds before the hunters and settlers killed them off – the buffalo, that is, not the Pawnee – although they did a number on them as well. Let's see if we can find anything in my research books to further classify this jewel," he said as he picked up the arrowhead and moved to the bookcase at the back of the room. He selected a rather thick volume and began to thumb through it, occasionally stopping to compare the arrowhead to pictures he located. "It's hard to be sure – there are no pure scientific methods to determine which tribe for sure carried this piece. Also, we can't determine the age since the various tribes passed down the art of chipping arrowheads from generation to generation. It could be quite old, but due to its good condition, I would guess it is not. Making arrowheads was a tedious and time-consuming task. Once fashioned, they were guarded with great care – some tribes even used them as part of their barter system. You know, ten arrows for a good horse, that sort of thing – and contrary to popular belief, the Indians did not rain arrows non-stop at their enemies. Even after a skirmish, the winners would carefully search the ground to retrieve any errant arrows. There was just simply too much invested in the making of arrowheads and arrows. You have to realize this really is just a piece of fairly hard rock that has been chipped and shaped into a point for a weapon. The tips were fairly fragile and would break easily when hitting a rock or even a bone. Consequently, the older an arrowhead, the more times the arrow had probably been used – the more times it had a chance to be broken."

"Here we go," said Mr. Kennedy. He had located a section about arrowheads and was closely comparing Ken's arrowhead to page after page of pictures of arrowheads. "It looks pretty close to this picture of a Kiota or maybe even this Morris arrowhead. It is quite possible this was an arrowhead made by the Pawnee tribe. Really in great shape," said the teacher.

Ken had begun to stare out the window as he again envisioned the history his area possessed. He blinked and realized Mr. Kennedy was waiting for him to respond to something. "I asked, have you found other artifacts in your exploration?" Mr. Kennedy repeated. Ken allowed that he had not and then asked, "These

Pawnee Indians you mentioned – how did they dress – what kind of clothing did they wear?"

"Well, they were quite similar to other tribes in that they had various types of garments depending on the occasion. Elaborate, colorful outfits for dances, quite bland animal skin loincloth breeches and so forth for everyday wear – let's see what we can find," he said as he located another thick book from his bookcase. He thumbed through the pages, murmuring to himself "no, no, not that, no, then perhaps like this," as he showed Ken a picture of an Indian brave on horseback with bow and arrow drawn in preparation of launching it into a large buffalo depicted on a dead run in the picture. The hunter had animal skin leggings with a strip of what looked like leather holding the leggings around his waist.

"Of course, that's just an artist's depiction of the Indian and his clothing."

Ken thought the Indian looked a lot like the Indian warrior he had seen in his vision the previous afternoon.

"Also," continued Mr. Kennedy, "the Indians depended more on buffaloes being stampeded over a cliff than trying to kill them with a bow and arrow. It would take a lot of arrows and time to kill a buffalo."

"How did they do it?" asked Ken.

"Well, the Indians followed the herds and knew where a number of buffalo jumps were located. When the herd neared one of the jumps, Indians mounted on horses would stampede the herd and try to head some of them over the jump. Sometimes a buffalo would fall and then others would trip and pile on the fallen.

Sometimes quite a number would be killed and the tribe would have an abundance of meat, hides and bones for their needs. The whole tribe would work to strip and butcher the downed buffaloes and replenish their food supplies for a number of months. If they did not get a lot of buffalo from the jump, they would inevitably get a few who would be downed and trampled in the course of the stampede. Many times the buffalo calves perished as did the older and less strong. Either way, the Indians relied heavily on the buffalo jump and stampede to provide their food."

"Did the Indians stampede the buffalo in this area?" asked Ken.

"I'm sure they must have at some point in history. There's even an old tale that they used a buffalo jump north of town two or three miles out near your dad's place."

The hair stood up on Ken's neck as he recalled his vision. "Did the Indians ever get hurt during the stampede?" asked Ken.

"Sure they did. It was a very dangerous thing they were doing. If they were caught in the stampede itself or if they lost their horses, it was almost certain death for them."

Ken knew he had witnessed a rare thing with his vision. He couldn't afford to tell anyone – who would believe a twelve-year-old boy anyway?

CHAPTER FOUR

Ken stood peering through the gate at the large house and spacious lawn area. Frost had come early that year and the pecan trees had produced a bumper crop. The crows were busy picking pecans from the loaded trees and cawing noisily at each other. Ken did a quick mental calculation: six pecan trees, fifty pounds of nuts per tree and an average of 30 cents per pound at the local produce store. If he could convince the owner to allow him to harvest the pecans and split the sale, he'd have more than enough for Christmas presents with maybe even enough left over for that model train set on display at Walker's department store. He had never had an electric train set and just knew he had to have it.

The house in front of Ken was larger than the average home in town, but was not the largest or most ornate. The doors and screens were in good condition although a couple of places appeared to be in need of some painting touch-up. The lawn was brown due to the heavy frost which caused it to die early. All in all, a very nice house but needing help in a few small areas.

Suddenly the side door to the house opened and a tall, rather thin man stepped out onto the porch carrying a briefcase. He turned and said he would be back next week, and stepped off the porch to the gray Chevrolet sedan parked in the driveway. The man wore horn-rimmed glasses and had prematurely thinning gray hair. He had an air of seriousness about him. As the car drove away, Ken opened the gate and walked slowly up the walk and the steps to the front door. He hesitated for a moment but after looking back at the crows fighting in the pecan trees, he turned and lifted the door knocker gently. No response. He lifted the knocker again, this time with a little more force. The door opened slightly and an elderly lady wearing bifocals peered down at Ken and asked in a mild voice, "Can I help you?"

"Yes ma'am," answered Ken. "I was just on my way back to school from lunch and noticed the fine crop of pecans your trees have produced." He motioned his hand toward the trees. The lady peered out at the trees then said, "Well, yes, so it seems." Ken stuck both hands in his pockets and asked, "Do you know how much those pecans are worth?" She looked again at the trees and back to Ken and said, "No, I really hadn't thought about it."

Ken started to tell her but thought that might be a little pretentious. After all, the way she had looked at the trees was like she hadn't even known she had pecan trees in her front yard. "Well, they're worth quite a bit but of course someone has to knock them down and pick them up and then take them to the produce store and sell them."

She looked at Ken for a moment and then said, "You wouldn't know anyone who could do all that would you?"

"Well, yes ma'am, I could do that and then we could split the money. Half for you as the owner and half for me for doing the work."

"What's your name?" she asked.

Ken stuttered out "Kenneth Bruce Adams."

She opened the screen door and extended her hand and said, "I'm Miss Kathy May Dillard. Why don't you come for tea tomorrow so we can discuss this business deal in detail."

"Tea, ma'am?"

"Yes, how about after you get out of school?"

"Well, yes ma'am, that would be fine – about 3:45, that's when I get out of school."

"Very well, Mr. Adams, I shall see you then."

Ken walked down the path and, as he closed the gate, took a look back at the house. Nothing was changed. But somehow, he felt someone was taking a long look at him too.

That evening, Ken shared his meeting with Miss Kathy May Dillard with his family during supper. After the full story, his father snorted, "I'm surprised she could even see you what with her nose so high – she can't even see the ground she walks on."

Ken wasn't sure exactly what his father meant – Miss Kathy May had certainly been able to see him and even the crows and pecan trees, although he did remember she had not seemed to really be aware of the trees before he called her attention to them. He whacked his younger brother Tommy and said, "Stop it." Tommy had been lightly kicking Ken's shins for the last few minutes knowing full well that no one could see what he was doing and hoping to get Ken into trouble as he no doubt had just accomplished.

"Don't you hit your brother again – you do that one more time and I'll take my belt to you," said his father.

Tommy's foot began the aggravation again – only slightly less forceful than before but with enough force for Ken to know it was not just an accident. Ken glowered at Tommy and hissed "Stop it" under his breath. Ken's mother reached under the table to squeeze Tommy's leg and said very quietly to him, "That's enough." Tommy sulked but at least he stopped kicking Ken in the shins. All the while, his father ignored the rest of them as he was absorbed in the country western music show on television. This had been a source of conflict ever since his father had purchased the television set. Try as his mother might, his father seemed to be drifting away from them as he had the TV on from the time he arrived home from work until he went to bed – generally to the din of the 10 o'clock news. He worked hard and did a good job at his office but they seemed less and less of a real family ever since the television set arrived. Of course, Tommy and Ken were not allowed to watch anything until after the supper dishes were done and any homework assignments completed. Mostly, they got the last half hour of the Edward R. Murrow report or some such show which was of no real interest to them. Ken's father dictated whatever was to be watched while his mother sewed or read some of her glamour magazines filled with stories of Hollywood starlets and film gossip.

Ken took advantage of a TV commercial and his father's break to inhale his dessert, and broached the subject of Miss Kathy May again. When he mentioned he thought he could make $40–$50 as his portion for harvesting the pecans, his father's ears seemed to perk up.

"That's a lot of pecans," he said.

"Yes, at least 300 to 400 pounds. It would probably take me two or three Saturdays to do them all but it would sure be worth it," Ken said.

"How are you planning to get them to the produce store?"

"Well, I was figuring we could get them into the trunk of your car and haul them over there," Ken said.

"Not so fast, not so fast. I may be doing something with Earl this weekend," his father said.

Ken's father's brother Earl was generally regarded as one step above snake spit by everyone except Ken's dad. Earl had never demonstrated a knack for much more than carousing, drinking and playing dominoes at the local pool hall. He had at one time managed to hold a job on a drilling rig for a sufficient length of time to get two fingers cut off his left hand. This feat had been accomplished by a drunk driller foreman who "threw the chain" onto the drill stem while Earl was in the process of fitting a section of pipe to the drill stem. The drilling company had provided Earl with a sizeable settlement in an effort to keep him from turning them in to the State Department of Exploration and Production.

It seems the company had garnered a reputation of much disrespect for the safety of their drilling practices. Earl had played this accident to secure a continued weekly payoff in the amount of $100. The drilling company didn't really care. They just continued to carry his name on the rig crew list and the paychecks just kept coming. All would be fine as long as he kept quiet and they just kept re-entering his name onto new rig lists as needed.

The next day, Ken could hardly wait for the bell to end Miss Dalton's sixth period English class. At last it rang and he dashed up the street toward Miss Kathy May's place and arrived sweaty and out of breath. The crows were still working at the pecan trees and Ken threw a couple of sticks at them in an effort to fight them off the prized booty. He waited at the steps for a minute to regain his breath then bounced up the steps and lifted the heavy knocker. It was a minute or two before the door opened and Miss Kathy May said, "Well, hello young man – you're right on time. Please come in."

The interior of the house was old – it looked old – all the furniture looked like it had been in the house for a hundred years. Ken later found out it wasn't quite that long, just fifty years.

Miss Kathy May asked him to join her in the parlor. She had a service set of cups with a small teapot and a plate of cookies set out. The furniture looked old to Ken. Old but of excellent quality. The parlor where they were sitting had two very large bookcases, both completely filled with books. More books than Ken had ever seen in a house. Certainly hundreds more than in his home. He wondered if Miss Kathy May had actually read all the books contained in the parlor. He noticed a number of titles seemed to be about American

Indians and many others about mineral exploration and refining. Others seemed to be about foreign countries. Ken was surprised at the number of framed photographs and documents displayed on the parlor walls. Most of them depicted young Native Americans proudly exhibiting various documents and awards. Miss Kathy May was included in some of the pictures but Ken could not make out the nature of the various awards and documents. There were quite a number of awards exhibited.

"How do you take your tea?" asked Miss Kathy May.

Ken was unprepared for the question – the only way he had ever had tea was over ice, which was how it was consumed at the Adams household year-round. "How do you take yours?" he asked.

"Oh, with a little sugar and just a hint of lemon," she replied.

"That sounds fine to me," he responded.

She poured the tea carefully into the cups, spooned in a half teaspoon full of sugar for each and then dipped a cut piece of lemon into the steaming tea for just a moment. She handed him a cup and saucer and asked if he would like a cookie. Ken responded "Sure." A growing boy of twelve could always take a cookie. He took two. They were a flavor he had not tasted before. He later learned they were made with oatmeal and raisins. The only way Ken had ever had oatmeal was at breakfast.

Miss Kathy May settled herself into a parlor chair and asked Ken to tell her a little about himself. Again, he wasn't prepared for her question. In his circle of adults, kids were pretty much told what to do and their opinions were not generally asked.

He stammered out something about his classes and family while she smiled and sipped her tea.

"And just how old are you, Mr. Adams?"

No one had ever addressed him as Mister before and it took a couple of seconds before he realized he hadn't responded to her question. "I'm twelve – twelve and a half," he responded.

She seemed to be looking far away and said very softly, "Yes, that would be about the same age."

"Same age as what?" he asked.

"Oh, something that happened a long time ago – happened to my poppa." Again she looked like she was seeing a world far away.

CHAPTER FIVE

Weatherford, Kansas   *March 1896*

The boy could hear the slaps and growls as his father administered another beating to his mother in the other room of the rundown shack. It always followed the same pattern – he would come home drunk and demand she cough up her little bit of money squirreled away from her butter and egg sales. She would protest that there wasn't any and the beating would start. Occasionally the beating stopped while he tore through the shack looking for her stash – if he found it, he would stagger out for more drink with his cronies down at the crossroads – if he didn't find it, the beating would resume until he passed out and fell to the floor.

With the tattered covers over his head, the boy did all he could to shut out the sounds but they couldn't totally be gone. This time he had had enough and he threw off the covers and lunged through the door just as his father had his hand drawn back ready to administer another round of slaps.

"Stop it!" he cried, louder than he had ever yelled in his life.

His father turned to him with a look of disbelief. The boy had never before had the courage to stand up to him, but at twelve and a half, he was large for his age and had developed good muscles in the previous year of hard work on the farm.

"What did you say?" his father sneered at him.

"Stop it!" the boy said, at which the father swung his fist at him with a glancing blow off his shoulder. Luckily, the drink and odd stance caused him to miss a direct hit on the boy's face and the father fell past him onto the floor. The boy leaped onto him and began pummeling his dad about the head, all the time yelling, "Never again, never again!"

The man threw the boy off into the wall and got to his knees at the same time trying to catch his breath. The boy was on him again like a terrier, yelling and hitting as hard as he could. Again, the man threw him off toward the wall and growled, "I'm gonna kill you and then I'm gonna kill her."

The boy felt the fireplace poker with his hand, grabbed it and swung with all his might in one long arching motion. The poker struck his father's skull with a loud crack, causing blood to spurt across the room. The man fell in a heap with no sign of movement. The boy looked at him in disbelief and then at his mother.

"I'm glad, I'm glad I did it," he said.

"Hush up," said his mother as she moved to the broken heap on the floor. She eyed the boy with wide eyes as she felt for a pulse in the man's neck.

"He's not dead," she announced. "You'll have to go – get away – go before he wakes up. When he wakes up he'll kill you."

"What about you? He'll kill you too."

"No, when he wakes up he'll be confused and I'll tell him he was beaten on his way home from the saloon. He'll be so confused maybe he won't even realize you're gone for a day or two. By that time you can be far enough away to be out of his life forever. When he's sober he doesn't beat me. It'll be a week or two before he works up enough gumption to go face his cronies. As bad as that head blow is, it may be a month. He's okay until he gets to drinking with them."

Again the boy asked, "What about you?"

"I can't leave," she said. "There's no place for me to go. I'm too old and broken to get out on my own. I have to stay."

With that, his tears began to flow, but there were no sobs – only deep breaths as she began to move toward the storage cabinet. Reaching behind, she extracted a small sack and emptied the handful of coins onto the bed. Quickly counting, she totaled up $6.40.

Handing the boy the money, she said, "Here, take it – you'll need help to get away." She was moving quickly around the room gathering odds and ends and rolling them into a knapsack.

"Here's a change of clothes with some cold chicken and hardtack biscuits. Don't tell me which way you're going. If he should wake up with any sense of what happened, I don't want to give him any help in trying to find you."

The boy jerked on his worn, thin shirt and jacket – grabbed the knapsack and bolted to the door. He stopped and looked back.

"I guess I never told you, but I love you," he said.

The tears slid down her cheeks. "I know," she said. "I know. Just take care of yourself and be honest and truthful, at least as much as you can without having to be brought back to this hell hole."

With that he dashed through the door and off down the road at a slow jog. He could maintain that rate for hours as he had done many times in the past on his way to school and back. The night was very dark yet he knew his way almost by instinct.

The boy was standing in line with a half dozen others anxiously looking at the group of men at the railroad construction site. The superintendent motioned to his foreman, "Give it to that chalk-headed kid, he looks strong enough to handle it."

The foreman motioned to the boy to join the group, "How about it kid, think you can keep water for a whole construction crew?"

The boy replied, "Sure I can do that just fine."

The foreman laughed, "Sounds simple huh? Wait till your tongue's hanging out from running fore and aft to a crew strung out a quarter of a mile down the track. You won't be doing much walkin'! What's your name anyway?"

The boy eyed the load of construction tools sitting on the flatcar and spotted one labeled Dillard and Sons, Chisels and Hammers.

"Didn't you hear me? What's your name?" demanded the railroad foreman.

"Dillard," the boy replied and looked him straight in the eye. "My name's Dillard."

"Dillard what?"

"Just Dillard," replied the boy. "That's all."

"Damndest thing I ever heard," said the foreman. "Everyone has at least two names. Hell I even knew a guy from Georgia had five names, all from fathers and grandfathers on both sides. I guess if he could have five names, you can get along with just one. But I'm gonna call you Chalk. With that head of chalk-colored hair, I'll never have to remember that other name, what was it now? Dillard? That's what I'm gonna put on the paymaster sheet – Chalk Dillard." However, he spelled it Chock.

And that's how Miss Kathy May Dillard's father acquired his name. For the rest of his life he was Chock Dillard. He never did tell anyone – not even her – his real name.

Chock had been carrying water for a week for the construction gang and he had learned most of the men's names and some background details on a few. The crew foreman, Ben, was his favorite as he exhibited the kind of leadership which resulted in respect from his men.

One day, Chock saw his father approaching down the line and he instinctively moved closer to Ben. His father was carrying a coiled whip over his shoulder, and a loose slouch hat covered the wound Chock had laid on his head with the fire poker.

His father stopped ten feet in front of him and hissed, "Git yourself over here. You got a little settling up coming for what you did to me."

"No, I'm never going back with you," said Chock.

Ben turned and stepped in front of Chock and said, "Now what's going on here?"

"That's my boy and I want him to come back to our shack right now."

"Is that right?" Ben asked Chock. "Yes, he's my old man but I'm never going back. I've seen him beat my ma too many times," said Chock.

"Is that right?" Ben asked Chock's father.

"What business is it of yours?" growled Chock's father as he uncurled his whip from his shoulder. "Now stand back or I'll give you a touch of this here black whip."

"That would be a very bad idea," said Ben.

At that, Chock's father snapped the whip back and curled a stroke toward Ben. Ben stepped forward and grabbed the whip with his left hand as his right pulled his long knife from his belt scabbard and he sliced the whip in two in one quick stroke of the knife. He grabbed the middle of the whip and sliced another three-foot-long section off with another stroke of his knife.

A couple of the railroad crew had gathered around to see what was happening and one of them picked up the two cut pieces of whip and tossed them toward Chock's father. "Now you better take your toys and go home," said Ben. "Don't come back here again.

We don't care much for wife beaters and you may have to be hauled off the next time you come," said Ben.

Chock's father picked up the pieces of his whip and shook them at Chock. "You caused this. Now I got two reasons to whip you." However, he was backing up and slowly turned around to proceed back the way he had come, occasionally looking over his shoulder with a sneer.

"If he comes back again, we'll get the company guards to haul him into court to face a judge for beating his wife," said Ben. "I bet he probably beat you too. I don't see how anyone would blame you for leaving that. Just remember, right can always stand up against evil and I believe your old man is evil."

Chock did not disagree.

CHAPTER SIX

Hendley, Texas   *Fall 1952*

It was Saturday morning and Ken was literally gulping down the breakfast his mother had served him. "Hey, slow down, you'll make yourself sick," said his mother.

"I need to get to town to harvest the pecans from Miss Kathy May's trees," said Ken. "It's going to take me today and next Saturday as well to get them all," he said.

"Well, you want to get there in a condition to be able to do it. Just slow down, they'll still be there," said his mother.

"Well, those crows steal some every day, pretty soon there won't be any pecans left if they keep it up, so I need to be going," said Ken as he put on his coat and cap. "I'll be home for supper." He gave his mother a hug on his way out the door.

"You be careful," she shouted to him as he mounted his bike and pedaled quickly down the road.

When he arrived at Miss Kathy May's walkway, he dashed up to the door and knocked with the heavy knocker. When Miss Kathy May opened the door, she said "My, my – you're early," to which Ken replied, "Yes, ma'am, but I want to get the first three trees done today and the next three next Saturday."

"You are a real charger," said Miss Kathy May. "Please be careful and do not get hurt."

"Yes, ma'am," replied Ken, and with that he was off to his first tree.

Ken climbed the tree quickly and began shaking and stomping on the tree limbs. The brown nuts rained down to the ground and soon it was practically covered with pecans. After he had finished with the shaking and stomping, he climbed down and began picking up the pecans and putting them into an empty coffee can he had brought along, then dumping them into one of two burlap feed sacks. His hands were quick and he had the ground cleared by mid-morning. He hoisted the first bag and figured he had about fifty pounds of nuts in it. He thought, "Boy, if the other trees are as good, we may get 300 pounds. That could result in $90 to be split fifty/fifty between myself and Miss Kathy May." That would be enough to cover his entire list of Christmas presents for his family members with enough left over for a special treat for himself.

Ken thought he might have seen a smiling face behind the window curtains once or twice while harvesting the pecans, but he wasn't sure. Maybe just a slight movement of the curtains.

He climbed the second tree and began the threshing process and again the nuts rained down. It was like music to his ears – the sound of money hitting the ground.

At noontime, Miss Kathy May called from the porch for Ken to take a break. She had two sandwiches ready along with a large glass of milk. Boy, did the sandwiches ever taste good.

She came back out onto the porch with a plate of cookies and asked if he would care for some. Ken took two.

"Well, it looks like you are making very good progress," she said.

"Yes, ma'am," Ken replied. "Got two done with four more to do. I'll get one more done today."

"That's pretty hard work for a young man your age. Are you sure you need to go that hard?"

"Yes, ma'am. Those crows are taking a toll on the trees, every day they pull away more and more so the sooner I get them down and to the store, the more money we will make."

"Well, tell me something about yourself," said Miss Kathy May.

Ken replied that he was in the seventh grade, liked math and history and really liked playing football on the Junior High team.

Miss Kathy May asked, "What position do you play?"

Ken replied, "Mostly flanker or end and sometimes punt returns."

"My, my," said Miss Kathy May with a questioning look at Ken as though she didn't know much about the game of football, let alone the various positions. "I had a boyfriend in school who played football," she said, "but that was a long time ago. His family moved away and we never saw each other after that."

Ken asked if she had lived in Hendley for a long time.

"Oh my, yes, I was born here. But that was a long time ago," she said.

CHAPTER SEVEN

Hendley, Texas   *Spring 1954*

Ken and his family were at the dinner table. His father took a break from the evening TV program and asked Ken how much longer before he reached summer vacation time from school.

"Two more weeks," advised Ken. "And that leads me to ask if you would be okay with me mowing people's lawns in town to make some extra bucks."

"You're big and strong and could probably do that," responded his father. "How would you do it?"

"Well, first off, I'd need to buy a mower, one that I could pull behind my bicycle. They've got some power mowers for sale at Bryman's Hardware. I checked them out the other day and there's one for $56 that would work great."

"Oh, yeah?" said his father. "And you'd pull it back and forth to town behind your bicycle?"

"No, I'll talk with Miss Kathy May and see if she'd let me store it and my tools in the shed where she parks her car. When I harvested pecans for her last year and the year before, she let me store them in her shed and there's lots of room in there. That way I won't have to bring the mower home after mowing people's lawns every day," replied Ken.

"Sounds like you have it all worked out."

"I could talk with her after school tomorrow and if she agrees, we could purchase the mower on Saturday and get everything set up," said Ken.

"Wait up there. This is your deal and you'll need to make your own arrangements to buy that mower," said his father.

"Okay, I will and I assume the overall plan is okay by you?" questioned Ken.

"Okay by me," his father replied.

The next day during lunch period, Ken hurried to Miss Kathy May's place, ran up the path and knocked on the door with the large brass knocker. Miss Kathy May opened the door and smiled at Ken.

"Now, what brings you to my porch this time of year? The pecans won't be ready to harvest until this fall," she queried.

"Yes, ma'am, I know," stated Ken. "I want to discuss a completely different idea with you but I don't have time to lay it all out before I have to get back to school."

"Can you come back for tea when school is out? We can discuss it then," she said.

"Great, I'll see you at 3:50 today."

At 3:50, Ken knocked on the front door for the second time that day.

"Please come in," said Miss Kathy May as she opened the door. "I have tea and cookies in the parlor."

Ken could not detect any changes to the house interior since his last visit the previous November.

"So what is this new endeavor of yours?" asked Miss Kathy May as she prepared the tea service in her normal fashion. Ken rapidly outlined his idea to offer lawn mowing services to the town's people. When he reached the end, he asked if she would allow him to store his mower and tools in her shed. Miss Kathy May smiled and said she was impressed with his plan and asked how long he thought he would offer his services.

Ken said, "As long as lawns need to be mowed, I will offer my services."

"You mean even through next summer and the summer after that?"

"Sure, even until I finish high school."

"Well, that certainly is an ambitious long-term plan. How did you come up with this plan?" asked Miss Kathy May.

"I was reading about the history of how some of the big businesses got started and they almost all started when a young guy had an idea on how to earn money, and started pursuing it. I realize that mowing lawns is not a long-term business to pursue, but for my age and location, I can make it work," said Ken.

"And I believe you will. You remind me somewhat of a friend my poppa had when he first came to this area. His friend's name was Ruell Pierce. Ruell first met my mother and her father. And then when he and my poppa met, they became friends for years," said Miss Kathy May.

CHAPTER EIGHT

Rural Texas   *Spring 1894*

The sun was hot and Ruell had been plowing the field since just after daybreak. As always, the mule pulling the plow had other ideas on how he intended to spend the day and pulling a plow was not at the top of his thinking. Ruell snapped the reins smartly, regained a degree of control and kept the plow going in a straight line. As they staggered forward, the mule began to compress his abdomen and Ruell knew immediately what was coming. The mule's anus rolled outward exposing the pink inside of his rectum followed by a loud WHOOSH. Ruell held his breath and was able to get the mule stopped, but too late – Ruell was engulfed in the stench of the mule fart. He eventually let his breath out and sucked in a long breath of foul odor. He retched and lost part of his lunch and with a second gag lost his balance. Bent over at the waist, hands on his knees, sucking air, coughing and spitting, he made his decision.

Ruell's father worked him and his brother like dogs. Morning, noon and night, they handled milking cows, slopping hogs, plowing and planting, seven days a week except they did not plow on Sundays. That was more to allow the mule to rest than for them. The farm barely made it by. On rare occasions their father did buy them some new clothes and work boots. However, there was never any money available for just pleasure. Their father was not really a bad man, but since their mother had died, he seemed only interested in working them to death.

Ruell unhitched the mule from the plow, much to the pleasure of the mule, and walked him back the quarter of a mile to his family's barn. He put the mule into his stall and added some oats to his feed trough. Ruell splashed water onto his face and arms before walking the short distance to his family's home. As he entered the back door into the screened-in porch, he could hear his younger brother and two sisters squabbling over whose turn it was to ride the homemade rocking horse.

"Quiet down you three, where's Pop?"

The three youngest were so surprised to see Ruell this early in the afternoon, they just stared and said nothing.

Again Ruell asked, "Where's Pop?"

Finally one of them said, "I think he said that he and Dan were going to go over to repair the fence line on the north forty."

Ruell moved to the room he shared with his older brother, grabbed a feed sack from under the bed and stuffed his few changes of clothing into the bag. His three younger siblings had observed the entire action from the doorway and asked, "What are you doing?"

As Ruell strode past them to the front room, he turned and said, "None of this is your fault – it's just time that I leave to find my own way."

At this, the three youngsters began to cry and asked, "Where will you go?"

"I don't know, just somewhere where I can have a chance to be something other than a dirt farmer. When Mama died and I had to quit school at the sixth grade to help here on the farm, it just seemed like I would be doomed to be a clod farmer all my life unless I got out. So now's the time." He bent down and gave each a hug and a kiss on the forehead. "In a couple of years you'll come to understand and you'll see why it has to be this way."

At that he pushed through the front screen door and headed purposefully in the direction he figured his father and brother would be working. Shortly, he saw them running a strand of barbed wire post to post. When he got to them, his father looked up and with surprise in his voice asked, "What are you doing here? There's another two to three hours of daylight left for you to plow the cornfield."

"I'm not plowing any more. The mule's in the barn and the plow's in the field. Dan can finish it out tomorrow," said Ruell.

"And where the hell do you think you're going?" asked his father.

"I don't know, just somewhere that I can have a chance to be something other than what I am here."

"Just gonna pull up and take off, just like that?" said his father.

"Sorry to leave you in a lurch but I've got to go. I've choked on my last mule fart and that's not the kind of life I want so I'm going." He turned to his brother, "Dan, I hope you make a go of it with Pops, he needs all the help you can offer."

With that said he turned to leave.

"If you walk away from this farm, don't ever plan to come back. The door won't be open to you," said Ruell's father.

"Don't worry, I'm not planning to come back," he responded as he crossed over the fence and continued in a western direction. His father and brother watched as his figure slowly melded into the prairie grass and brush.

The next day, Ruell was on his knees moving slowly toward the range rabbit. He hurled the rock with his right hand and it flew true and hard, striking the rabbit in the head, knocking it senseless.

At dusk, he turned the rabbit slowly on the spit over the small fire and it smelled great. He had had nothing to eat since he said goodbye to his former life on the farm and he was so engrossed in the cooking that he failed to hear the two riders as they approached his campsite. When he did notice the two horses with their riders curiously watching him, he jumped back from the rabbit with a start.

"Careful now, you'll knock that rabbit into the fire and all of us will go hungry," said the taller of the two riders as he dismounted from his horse. He was definitely a cowboy with a wide-brimmed hat, neck kerchief, leather vest and a large pistol holstered in a heavy gun belt.

"My name's Russ and this here," pointing at his sidekick, "is Muley. We're riding point for Mr. Anderson's herd and taking it to the stockyards at Amarillo. We've got a half dozen pieces of hardtack to gnaw on and they sure would go well with a piece of that rabbit," said Russ. "How about we share our hardtack biscuits with you for a couple of pieces of your rabbit?"

"Sounds good to me," said Ruell. He took the rabbit off the fire, pointed it at Russ and said, "Grab that leg and I'll cut it off." As he pulled his knife from his belt, the cowboy's hand moved to the butt of his pistol and he said easily, "Just make it a nice slow cut. You wouldn't want to slip and cut yourself."

Ruell slowly sliced off the rabbit leg. "How about you?" he asked as he pointed the rabbit carcass toward Muley.

"Sure just like with Russ, nice and slow."

Russ turned to open his saddlebag and extracted a small sack which contained the six pads of hardtack, handing two each to Muley and Ruell. They all squatted down around the fire and ate in silence. Eventually, Russ asked Ruell, "What you doing out on this prairie? There's nothing within twenty miles of here except sagebrush, jackrabbits and rattlesnakes."

Ruell had no idea how far he had traveled since saying farewell to his family. "I decided to leave the farm and try my hand at something else – something I haven't done before. Do you ever use that thing?" he asked Russ as he pointed at the pistol.

"Sure. We occasionally have to shoot a snake or coyote trying to steal young calves," said Russ.

"Or sometimes a wandering polecat," added Muley. "You know polecats come in many different sizes and some can be downright cantankerous." At this both cowboys laughed. "How about you? You ever have to shoot a polecat?" asked Muley.

"Heck no, I've never shot anything," responded Ruell. "I've never even shot a pistol."

For some reason this sent the cowboys into hysterics, laughing and slapping their thighs. Finally they stopped laughing and asked, "Do you know how to ride a horse?"

Ruell replied he had never ridden a horse, which set the cowboys off again. When they regained their breaths and asked, "Do you know how to rope?" Ruell replied that roping, too, he did not know how to do. Again this resulted in another round of howls and laughter. Finally, wiping tears from their eyes, one of the cowboys asked, "Just what do you know how to do?"

"I know how to plow with a mule," Ruell replied.

At that the cowboys howled and rolled in the prairie grass. As Ruell watched, he too began to laugh and soon all three were whooping and wiping tears from their eyes. Finally, Russ said, "We're gonna have to take you back to the herd with us. We'll teach you how to be a cowboy, 'cause a cowboy can do damn near anything because he has to, to be able to stay alive."

Ruell and Muley rode double on the horse the next morning as the three of them joined up with the herd. They sought out Mr. Anderson riding near the front of the herd.

"We got a real greenhorn here but we couldn't leave him wandering around on the prairie," said Russ. "Hope it's alright that we brought him along."

Ruell dismounted from Muley's horse and said, "He's right but I'm willing to work and learn."

"What can you do?" asked Mr. Anderson.

At this, the two cowboys howled with laughter and wheeled their horses around toward the chuck wagon in hopes of getting something to eat. Mr. Anderson stared after them as Ruell turned red with embarrassment.

"I guess about all I know how to do is plow fields and bust clods," said Ruell.

"Well, we don't need anyone to do that for us. Cows don't know nothing about clods," said Mr. Anderson. "How about helping out with the cook? You can carry water and make coffee can't you?"

"Yes, sir, I can do that and like I said, I learn fast," said Ruell.

"Well, head back to the chuck wagon and tell Tom that I said it was okay for you to come along with us. We're still seven to eight days from Amarillo and we'll see what happens after that," said Mr. Anderson.

Ruell walked through the dust and cattle till he met up with the chuck wagon where he introduced himself to the man handling the reins and told him what Mr. Anderson had said.

"Well, okay, throw your sack up here and you can share this seat with me. It sure beats walkin,'" said Tom.

As the chuck wagon jolted along, Ruell learned that the herd consisted of approximately 4,000 head of cattle with eight drovers to move them along. They had been on the trail for a week making eight to ten miles per day. Tom shared that he had worked for Mr. Anderson for four years all as a cook and general assistant. He was the one the cowboys came to with their complaints or requests and he forwarded the information to Mr. Anderson. They had a respectful relationship and it was Tom who generally acted as a buffer between the crew when some sort of dispute erupted, which was not often but seemed to become more frequent the longer the trail drive lasted. This was the second trail drive Tom had been on with the Lazy L Ranch.

The first one three years before only had approximately 3,000 head of cattle and lasted four weeks. During that drive, they experienced rain, hail and general discontent with three or four good fistfights but no killings. Tom wore a revolver the same as the other cowboys, "to shoot snakes and coyotes," he said, but with no mention of polecats. Ruell asked if he could examine Tom's sidearm as he had never held one before. He was surprised at how heavy it was but strangely more confident when he had the gun in his hand. It had the name Colt .45 machined into the base of the revolver and Tom explained that it was the model favored by most of the cowboys. It had cartridges sufficiently powerful to do significant damage when hitting the target, whereas a lighter gun such as a .32 or .38 caliber would do less damage. The lower-caliber guns were lighter and easier to carry but were not respected like the .45 caliber was.

Furthermore, the .45 pistol and Winchester saddle gun could both fire the same cartridges, which meant it was far more convenient since the cowboy did not have to carry two different types of cartridges for his weapons.

Ruell handed the pistol back to Tom who put it back into his holster and moved the keeper loop over the hammer. He explained to Ruell that this kept the gun from coming out of the holster if the cowboy had to ride over rough ground or chase an ornery cow through the brush.

"Maybe sometime you could show me how to shoot," said Ruell.

"Sure, we'll get somewhere on the trail after the herd is sold and I'll show you. Don't want to do any shooting near the cattle as it could cause them to stampede and that's how cowboys sometimes get killed," said Tom.

Tom moved the chuck wagon on ahead of the herd and located a flat clear area near a running stream. They halted the wagon, unleashed the team of horses and applied their hobble ropes to keep them from wandering off during the night.

Tom told Ruell to check the water in the stream to see if it was fit to drink and if so to bring two or three containers full to the wagon. The wagon had a large water barrel attached to the side near the front. Tom instructed Ruell to place the containers under the wagon.

Tom was quick to get a fire going and set a small cast-iron kettle partially filled with water on the fire. He added about a half gallon of beans to the pot when it began to boil. He then extracted a cured ham from the wagon stores, cut it into chunks and added it to the beans. He retrieved a Dutch oven cooker from the wagon and set it up near the rear of the fire. He took out an earthen crock with a glob of dough at the bottom. He quickly pulled off about a fourth of the blob and began forming the dough into pads about an inch in diameter. He placed these onto a metal sheet and set the sheet into the Dutch oven.

"These will be ready in about twenty minutes. Hardtack biscuits," he advised Ruell. "A cowboy's staple. Beans, ham and hardtack. We'll add a little more salt, flour and water to the base before bedtime and it'll be ready for another round in the morning. Just need to keep the hardtack base fed and it'll last for months," said Tom.

"Take those cans of stream water and set them near the fire," instructed Tom. "Bring the water to a boil and then put them back under the wagon. In the morning when the water has cooled down, scoop off the top half or so and add it to the water barrel. That way, we replenish our water and never run out," he added. There was more to learn about this cowboying then Ruell had realized.

CHAPTER NINE

Amarillo, Texas   *April 1894*

T he crew herded the cattle into holding pens at the railroad stockyard. They filled most of the available pens. Ruell was fascinated by the counter man. He sat on a post as the cattle were channeled through a chute and he kept a running count as well as the various brands. When finished, he reported to Mr. Anderson: "I got 3,858 Lazy L, 115 for the J&J and 112 for the Curly C."

"Sounds about right to me," said Mr. Anderson. "I'll see that the money gets passed on to the rightful owners."

Ruell learned this was standard practice when rounding up ranch cattle. It was normal that a few cattle from neighboring ranches got mixed in with the rancher's spread. The owners of the J&J and the Curly C would probably end up with some Lazy L cattle when they took their herds to market. At the going rate of $40 per head, this was a sizeable sum.

Mr. Anderson took his bill of sale to the local Bank of North Texas to deposit, and withdrew sufficient cash to pay off the crew as well as enough to cover his expenses for the coming return trip to his ranch. After paying off the crew, everyone except Ruell and Tom headed for Saloon Alley.

Mr. Anderson allowed that some of them would drift back to the ranch after a week or so of drinking, gambling and whoring. They'll be mostly broke and looking to sign on for another year of work. Tom asked Mr. Anderson to take a look at the rear axle on the chuck wagon. It had seemed wobbly for the last few miles of the cattle drive. As Mr. Anderson crawled under the rear of the wagon, he told Tom to give the wagon a good shake, which he did, and the back left wagon wheel collapsed.

"Help me," yelled Mr. Anderson, "I'm pinned under here."

Tom and Ruell grabbed Mr. Anderson's legs and pulled as hard as they could but to no avail. "You pull while I lift," said Ruell to Tom.

Ruell placed his back against the rear of the wagon, squatted down about four inches, grabbed the underside of the wagon and lifted. His eyes felt like they would pop out of his head and his forehead throbbed like crazy. He had always been big and strong for his age. Now his body was straining with all his might to help save a man's life. Tom dragged Mr. Anderson clear of the wagon and Ruell lowered it back to the ground.

They helped Mr. Anderson to his feet as he dusted off his jacket and pants.

"Are you okay? Any broken bones?" asked Tom.

"I don't think so, just smashed up and bruised a bit," replied Mr. Anderson, adding, "I've never seen anything like that. That wagon must weigh over a thousand pounds."

"Well, it's a good thing I didn't have to lift the whole thing," said Ruell.

"Even so, you must have lifted 300 or 400 pounds," said Tom.

"I'm just glad I could do it," said Ruell.

Mr. Anderson turned to Ruell, stuck out his hand and said, "I owe you a lot, that thing could have crushed me pretty bad. I think my ranch needs someone like you. You stay with me and I'll see that you learn everything I know about ranching and cattle. The pay's only $50 a month but in a few years you could become a foreman and that pays $100 a month.

Tom was grinning ear to ear and said, "I'll teach you everything I know about cooking, and that will take at least a day or two!" The three of them had a good laugh at that.

After having the wagon repaired, Mr. Anderson told Tom and Ruell to go to the general market and stock up on supplies for the ranch. He had already paid for the supplies and had ordered six rolls of barbed wire as well as staples, nails, hammers and various other necessary tools. After they loaded the wagon, they started the long drive back to the ranch. Mr. Anderson said he would follow in a few days as he had some other business to attend to while in Amarillo.

At the first campsite, Tom and Ruell set up camp and cooked a simple meal for the two of them. After cleaning up, Ruell asked

Tom if he was any good with his pistol. Tom allowed that he could hold his own and also informed Ruell that he had never pulled his gun against another man. Ruell asked if Tom could demonstrate how to use his pistol and he said, "Sure, let's go down a piece so the noise won't frighten the horses and I'll show you."

The two walked away from the wagon, found a dry stream bed, and Tom instructed Ruell to go pick up a half dozen or so rocks about fist size and set them up some twenty-five to thirty paces downstream. Ruell did as instructed and returned to stand by Tom. Tom extracted his pistol, spun the cylinder and checked that he had all six chambers loaded. He then turned sideways and lifted the pistol to sight down the barrel. The first shot was really loud and the bullet kicked up sand about a yard in front of the first stone. The second shot missed to the left by about twelve inches. The third again hit a foot in front of the stone. The fourth shot went high and the bullet hit the ground twenty feet behind the stone. Tom lowered the pistol and stared at the rocks and said, "It's harder than it looks. You want to take a shot?"

"Sure," said Ruell as he took the pistol from Tom, imitated his stance, sighted down the gun barrel and took aim. He squeezed the trigger slowly as Tom had instructed and was surprised at the kick of the pistol as the bullet hit eighteen inches in front of the stone. He took aim again and held the pistol steadier than before. When the pistol fired, the rock burst into flying chunks. Tom blinked, sucked in his breath and said, "Holy cow, your second shot hit the mark straight on. You sure you never fired a pistol before?"

Three days later, Mr. Anderson caught up with them having concluded his business in Amarillo. "Bought a dozen new Herefords to give a try on the range. They'll be arriving in about a month," Mr. Anderson said. "We'll see how well they fare with the longhorns. They look like they have better cuts and could add as much as twenty percent more weight per animal. They're going at $80 per head so it makes sense to give them a try."

"Have to see how well they handle a winter with snow and sleet," Tom said.

A few days later they arrived at Mr. Anderson's ranch and were greeted by Manuel and Maria and Mr. Anderson's daughter, Mary. Ruell was surprised to see the twelve-year-old Mary acting like she was in charge, but in fact, she pretty much had been while her father was away on the cattle drive. Manuel was the house man and his wife was the housekeeper and cook. They had been with Mr. Anderson for twelve years, ever since Mary's mother had died while giving birth. Mary gave Tom a hug and called him an old reprobate, which meant nothing to Ruell but Tom laughed and said she should have better manners seeing how she was preparing to be sent to finishing school down in Houston.

Tom turned her to Ruell and introduced them. Ruell could just barely mumble, "Pleased to meet you," as he stared at the ground and shifted sand with his foot. She laughed and stuck out her hand to shake, at which Ruell dropped his hat he had been holding with both hands in front of his torso. Turning red in the face, he stooped to pick up his hat all the while attempting to shake her extended hand.

"Don't worry," said Tom, "we'll drive some proper manners into him and someday he may even manage a dance with you!"

"That would be nice," stated Mary as she turned to dance up the stairs.

Ruell was completely dumbstruck as he watched her retreat into the house. He thought she was just about the most amazing person he had ever met.

"Come on, let's get you set up with a bunk in the bunkhouse," said Tom.

The next day, Mr. Anderson instructed Tom and Ruell to hitch up the surrey so he could take Mary and Maria into Hendley to catch the stage. Maria would accompany Mary to the finishing school in Houston, get her set up and established and then return to the ranch in a couple of weeks. In the meantime, Tom would handle the cooking at the Big House and the bunkhouse as well, with Ruell's help. Ruell learned quickly and soon could put a fairly decent meal together for the few cowboys who had slowly drifted back to the ranch pretty much as Mr. Anderson had predicted.

Six weeks later, Russ, Muley, Ruell and three others on the crew took a trip to move part of the remaining herd to fresh pastureland on the other side of the ranch.

They had halted for the day and gathered around the campfire to have their evening meal of beans with ham chunks and hardtack biscuits, the standard trail meal.

"Well now," said Hack, one of the coarser herders as he ladled a generous dipper of beans and ham onto his plate, "you gonna get a cake for your birthday or just another plate of beans? Ha, you'll be getting a piece of cake alright," he said, just as he raised his right leg and blew a huge fart in Ruell's direction.

"Leave him alone," said Russ, sitting off to one side looking down at his plate as he slowly chewed his dinner.

Hack cocked his head toward Russ and drew his lip into a tight sneer. "This ain't none of your business," he snarled. "Maybe it's just time that little Ruell boy here learns how the real world works."

"And how's that?" asked Russ, again just real quiet and still not even looking at Hack.

"Like knowing whose ass to kiss and when – knowing how to get ahead in the world – knowing how to be a straw boss foreman for one thing," snarled Hack at Russ.

The air was so still you could hear the insects buzzing – no one moved – no one breathed.

"Well, now, I reckon you could show us all a thing or two yourself," replied Russ, still not looking up or even acknowledging the insult. "You could probably even kick my ass seeing how young and strong you are. Hell, yes, you could do that. But then I'd have to have the marshal swear out a warrant for your arrest for an unprovoked fight. I do believe a jury would find you guilty what with all these witnesses sitting around here and willing to tell the truth in court. They'd probably send you up to that territorial prison in Leavenworth. Now they've got some real badasses up there. I figure what with your mouth running off the way it does, they'd cut your guts out within a month or two. And you know that cemetery on the other side of the prison? When I go up there next spring I'd go over and hunt up your grave and I'd just have the biggest old smile on my face while I stand there pissing on your grave." At which point he lifted his head to give Hack the biggest, widest smile Ruell had ever seen. The vessels pumped and throbbed in Hack's forehead – his eyes bulged and he uttered small groaning sounds as he stood up – threw his remaining food in the fire and stomped away.

Everyone breathed a sigh of relief and looked at each other. You could hear the snapping sounds as hidden pistol hammers were released.

Ruell realized he had just seen the value of winning a fight with brains rather than fists.

CHAPTER TEN

Anderson Ranch, Texas   *Spring 1902*

M r. Anderson handed Ruell a bank draft and said, "Take this into town to the bank to draw this month's payroll for the ranch hands. Five hundred should cover it with some left over for the safe."

With that, Ruell rose from his chair and headed for the foreman's room at the rear of the bunkhouse.

"Billy, go and saddle my mare for my trip into town," instructed Ruell as he entered the bunkhouse. There were four cowboys including Russ, Muley and two new hands playing cards at one of the tables.

"Hurry back with that payroll," said Russ. "Muley's already down $10 and he needs his pay to square up."

"You guys shouldn't be playing on credit," said Ruell. "It only leads to trouble and the next time there's a bust-up inside the bunkhouse, Mr. Anderson will ban any future gambling."

"We know, we know," said Russ and Muley at the same time. "Won't be no bust-up today."

"Okay guys, let's just switch to matches to keep score," said Russ.

At that, Ruell grabbed his hat and saddlebags and headed for the door just as Billy came back in.

"You're all set. I made sure she got a drink before saddling up. She's all fresh and ready to go," said Billy.

"Thanks, see you guys this afternoon," said Ruell and swung himself up into his saddle. He turned the mare toward the lane and began a slow trot to Hendley. The trip would require three hours each way.

Ruell hummed to himself as the mare trotted at a steady pace, which he knew she could maintain for hours, although he occasionally stopped to allow her to catch her breath.

He entered the outskirts of the town and noted a half dozen new homes were under construction as well as a new blacksmith's shop and horse stable. He was proud the town was prospering and had recently completed a new three-room schoolhouse.

Shortly, he arrived at the bank, tied his horse to the hitching rail, grabbed his saddlebags and entered the building.

"Morning Miss Bailey," he said as he tipped his hat to an elderly lady who was just leaving the bank.

"Good morning, Mr. Pierce. You're in for the ranch payroll?"

Ruell nodded and was glad no one else was in the bank to be made aware that he would soon have a sizeable sum of money in his saddlebags. He held the door for her and turned toward the teller's cage to conduct his business. He handed the bank draft to the teller and passed his saddlebags over the counter to him.

"Please make it mostly ones, tens and twenties," Ruell said.

The teller nodded and said, "This is for the ranch payroll?" Ruell nodded and said hello to Jack Barton, the Bank Manager. "How're things going at the ranch?" asked Jack.

"Pretty well. The new breed of cattle Mr. Anderson brought into the ranch has adapted well and it looks like they will be the dominant breed within the next eight to ten years. They have about twenty percent more meat per steer versus the longhorns that Mr. Anderson started with."

At that, the teller said, "Everything's set, just sign this receipt and you'll be on your way."

Two more customers had entered the bank and Ruell turned with his saddlebags and was almost to the door when three masked robbers with guns drawn entered the bank.

"Everyone on the floor!" they yelled. "I'll take that," said one as he grabbed the saddlebags from Ruell. "Everyone on the floor!" they yelled again.

Ruell lay down flat on his stomach with his hands stretched out in front as did the other customers. One of the robbers vaulted over the bank banister and stuck his gun under Jack Barton's chin and said, "You've got one minute to get that safe open or you're a dead man."

Jack kneeled in front of the safe, spun the dials and the tumblers clicked into place. He swung the safe open, stood up and stepped back from the safe.

The robber swung a set of saddlebags from his shoulder at Jack and said, "Fill it up, fast."

Jack kneeled at the safe and began pulling stacks of bills from inside and sticking them into the saddlebags. Ruell was angry at his inability to do anything about the robbers. He had been trusted to bring the payroll funds to the ranch and now they were being stolen from him along with all the cash from the bank. He clenched and unclenched his fists with his arms stretched out on the bank floor. The second robber had holstered his gun and was going through the pockets of Ruell and the customers lying on the floor. The robber with the saddlebags filled with the bank cash yelled "Here" as he tossed the saddlebags to the second robber now at the teller's cage. The third had been acting as a lookout near the door and the second robber yelled "Catch" as he tossed Ruell's saddlebags to the lookout.

As they spun through the air, the robber tried to holster his pistol but missed his holster and the gun clattered to the floor directly in front of Ruell. It seemed like everything was moving in slow motion as Ruell grabbed the gun, rolled on the floor, shot the robber at the teller's cage and also shot the first robber as he was vaulting over the bank banister. The lookout started to run to the door when Ruell tripped him and down he went. Ruell was on him in a flash and knocked him cold with the pistol he had just grabbed from the floor.

Slowly, the customers, teller and bank manager got to their feet.

The teller said, "Holy shit, did you see that?" The teller kneeled beside the two shot robbers, felt for a pulse and finding none, said, "They're both dead."

At that moment, the local Sheriff rushed through the door saying, "What's going on in here?" He stopped to stare as the teller announced, "They were holding up the bank and Ruell shot these two and cold-cocked that one over there," pointing to the previous robber lookout. "Holy shit, never seen anything like that before," said the little teller.

"Where did you learn to shoot like that?" asked Jack Barton.

"I taught myself, out on the range over the years. Never thought I'd ever shoot anyone though," said Ruell.

Well, that was pretty fast action being surrounded by three armed robbers at the same time," said the Sheriff. "If you ever have a desire to be a lawman, I'd sure be pleased to have you as a Deputy and in a year or two when I retire, you could take my place. I'm getting too old to try and keep up with these young bucks. Looks like you could handle it with no problem," he added.

Ruell thought about what the Sheriff had said on his way back to the ranch. He had worked to develop his shooting capabilities until he could shoot a tossed half dollar out of the air at twenty paces. He could draw and shoot accurately in a split second too. He figured if he did become a lawman, his reputation for having killed the two bank robbers plus his shooting prowess would discourage most, if not all, of the men trying to cause his county any trouble. Besides, he was tiring of the rigors of ranching. It was hard, hot, dusty work and all he could see in his future was more of the same. Mr. Anderson's son would become the ranch manager after Mr. Anderson handed down the reins.

When he reached the ranch, he passed his mare off to a ranch hand and marched into the Big House with the saddlebags and the payroll funds. After he told Mr. Anderson what had happened at the bank, Mr. Anderson, as well as Manuel and Maria, were amazed and they all looked at him in a different way. Ruell felt more mature than when he had left for the bank that morning. Prior to that time, Ruell had not carried a pistol on his person. Now, however, he sensed that he should. He had no idea who the bank robbers were. Did they have other partners or relatives who might want to settle their anger toward him for killing two of them and putting the third into jail? Ruell had no idea.

A week later, the Sheriff rode up to the ranch and asked to speak with Ruell. He advised he had not seen any new suspicious men in town but he did have other good news.

"Sent out a wire on those three robbers last week and just got the response this morning. Seems like they had earned themselves quite a reputation for robbing banks. Wells Fargo has posted a reward of $1,000 each for those three upon their death or being convicted at trial. The Wells Fargo people are sending a special agent down to investigate and if they concur in the identity of these three yahoos, you'll be rewarded the $3,000. You'll be rich!"

"That's all well and good," replied Ruell, "but I would rather know if anyone's going to be coming by with an intent to revenge their friends or relatives."

"Don't know anything in that regard. I'd just lay low at the ranch for a while and see how it plays out."

"No, I think I'd rather be in town to see them first. Does that offer to be a Deputy still stand even after the reward and all?"

"It sure does, when would you want to start?"

"I'll need to square everything with Mr. Anderson. He has been very fair and good to me. I want to let him know how much his help has meant to me."

"That wouldn't also have anything to do with his daughter, Mary, now would it?" asked the Sheriff with a smile.

Ruell's ears and neck reddened as he grinned back at the Sheriff. "Yeah, I want to ask Mr. Anderson if his Mary could become my Mary," said Ruell as the Sheriff mounted his horse for the ride back to Hendley.

Ruell knocked on Mr. Anderson's office door.

"Come in," responded Mr. Anderson as he laid down a cost ledger he had been reviewing. "What is it Ruell?"

Ruell stood before the desk holding and turning his hat with both of his hands. "I spoke with the Sheriff this morning, and he advised there was a sizeable reward posted for those three robbers as they had robbed other banks as well. I also spoke with him about becoming his Deputy and eventually running for Sheriff when he retires. I'd like to have your okay on that as you have treated me good and fair since the first day you hired me."

"Well, you're a capable grown man and you don't need my okay to change careers, but we sure will miss you around here," he said sincerely.

"Well, there's another thing I will need your permission for and that is to call on your Mary. I truly love her and want to do everything in my power to make her happy and hopefully someday convince her to marry me."

"Now, as you well know, Mary's a strong, independent young woman. She makes her own decisions so I would suggest you set up your own arrangement with her as anything I directed her to do wouldn't be listened to anyway," replied Mr. Anderson. "As to marriage, time will tell. If she should come to love you then I would not object. I'll worry about your decision to become a lawman. There are more bad people in the world than I care to admit but I trust your judgment and wish the best for you in your future."

Ruell's knees were shaking as he stumbled through the door. He felt his life had just taken a major change for the better.

CHAPTER TWELVE

R uell was sitting at the Sheriff's desk completing his monthly reports on local criminal activity when the Sheriff entered the office. Ruell began to rise and the Sheriff said, "No, no, go ahead and keep your seat. God knows you have been more of a Sheriff than a Deputy for the past year and a half and done a fine job of it too. I've decided you should enter the race to take my place in November and become the rightful Sheriff of this county. I'll do all I can to help and I'll introduce you to all my backers and I'm sure they will welcome you to take my place."

"Well, that's right kind of you, Sheriff. My Mary and I have discussed this possibility in detail a number of times and she's in favor of it too," replied Ruell. "My Mary is scheduled to travel to the clinic in St. Louis for a round of tests. She has experienced some minor health problems and we want her to get checked out if for no other reason than to relieve our concerns. I won't make a final decision on running for Sheriff until she returns from the consultation in a couple of weeks, if you don't mind."

Two weeks later, Mary arrived by stage. She was met by Ruell as the driver handed down her bag and valise.

"So good to see you, my love," breathed Ruell as he held her in his arms. "How was the examination?" he asked.

"Let's discuss this at home," she replied, without meeting Ruell's questioning eyes.

They rode home in silence and after entering their home, Mary sat down on the parlor divan and began to sob softly. Ruell was at her side immediately.

"What is it, what did they say?" questioned Ruell.

"The doctors said I will never be able to provide you with a child, there is nothing they can do to change it. My body is not made right," she sobbed. "There is nothing either of us did to cause this, it is just the way my organs were formed. There's nothing they can do," at which she collapsed completely into Ruell's arms, sobbing uncontrollably.

"Now, now, it's okay, we'll adopt or somehow get to have children in our lives, some way, somehow."

"I should just run away and give you a chance to have someone else who can give you children."

"Now stop that, I don't want anyone else, ever. We're committed to each other for the rest of our lives, no matter what. Remember those vows we said on our wedding day? For richer or poorer, in sickness and in health for the rest of our lives till death us do part. I meant that and I believe you did too so let's just take a deep breath, make adjustments in our plans and expectations and go on from there."

It was two weeks before Ruell mentioned his talk with the Sheriff regarding running for office, and Mary asked, "Is that what you want to do?"

Ruell responded, "Yes, I've been handling the bulk of the responsibility of the job for the better part of the past year and people seem to respect the way I have handled it. The pay is not real great but we still have some of the reward money from the bank robbery and we'll be just fine. So, yes, I want to do it."

"Then let's do it right. What can I do to help?" Mary asked.

Ruell campaigned honestly and diligently. He was elected in a landslide and he and Mary moved into the town of Hendley. Mary got a job teaching at the growing school and they settled into a modest but well-respected life.

CHAPTER THIRTEEN

Hendley, Texas   *Spring 1905*

C hock was running behind schedule and the dirt road
conditions were certainly not helping. Recent rains had left
a series of ruts, making it impossible to make up any lost time. Even
so, he urged the 1904 Runabout to the maximum speed possible on
the stretches that were not too badly eroded. As he rounded a turn,
the ruts were especially deep and a large rock had been exposed in
one of the ruts his wheels occupied. He did not see the rock in time
to avoid the substantial jolt as the front wheel absorbed the full
force of the encounter. The wheel tie rod bent and threw the car
into a severe skid over to the side of the road.

As Chock surveyed the right front wheel turned inward
at an odd angle, he knew his schedule now completely
shot and it would be impossible to make the monthly District
Manager's meeting that Monday afternoon. He kicked the tire in

discouragement, drew back and took a look down the road. Off to the right about a quarter mile sat an orderly looking farmhouse surrounded by cool shade trees. By the time Chock reached the driveway, he had become well aware of the heat of the noonday sun. The porch on the farmhouse provided welcome relief from the heat as he knocked on the screen door.

"May I help you?" came the reply behind the screen and Chock could not clearly make out the person standing in the shadows of the entry room. The voice was obviously feminine, but any more than that he could not discern. He gave a quick rundown of his predicament, closing with a request asking if someone could give him a lift into town to engage the services of a mechanic to repair his car. The screen door opened slightly and he could now see it was a young woman in a cool summer dress who responded that her father was due from the fields at any moment for his noontime meal and she was sure he would be able to help.

"Thank you very much, and if you don't mind, would it be all right for me to wait for him in the shade on the porch?" Chock asked.

The young woman said that would be fine and closed the door as she stepped back into the room which again obscured his vision of her.

Chock sat down on the porch step and mopped at his brow with his handkerchief. Shortly, he heard the screen door open as the young woman emerged with a pitcher and two glasses.

"Perhaps you would like some lemonade while you wait," she said.

Chock stood up and took the glasses while she poured the lemonade.

"It's much cooler in the swing on the porch, won't you join me?"

Stuttering, Chock replied, "Why, yes, yes, I'd like that." He noted she had sun-bleached hair and blue eyes as well as an appealing figure.

"My name is Sara May Miller, please have a seat," she gestured toward the swing.

Chock stammered out his name and said he worked for the railway all the while looking at Sara May as though he had never seen a woman before, at least not one that looked as pretty and who seemed to smile all the time.

As they sipped their lemonade, she told Chock that she had recently left college to come home to assist her father with his farm and home. Her mother had passed away recently and she felt it was necessary that she be there for her father as her parents had been happily married for twenty-eight years.

Chock was simply mesmerized by the ease at which she described these events in her life which could cause others to simply grieve and fade away.

Soon, Sara May's father came through the house and out onto the porch. Sara May introduced her father, Brad Miller, and Chock outlined his dilemma. Brad asked Chock to join them for lunch and then he would give him a ride into town. Sara told them to wait outside while she fixed a plate of sandwiches and another pitcher of lemonade.

Chock and Brad eased down onto the porch swing and each took a sandwich from the plate. It was one of the best sandwiches Chock had ever had and he told Sara May so.

"It's the bread – it's her own recipe," said Brad. "Her mother taught her the recipe and I swear she could make a business just selling her own homemade bread loaves."

Sara May simply smiled and said she was glad they were enjoying the sandwiches. While Chock enjoyed another sandwich, Brad finished his glass of lemonade.

"Well, he said, let's get you to town so you can get someone to come get that car of yours. Can't leave it out on the road all day."

Sara said goodbye to the two men as they bumped down the driveway in Brad's old truck.

"Your daughter served a nice lunch – great lemonade too," said Chock.

Brad simply gave him a sideways glance and said nothing.

"She certainly knows how to put a person at ease," continued Chock.

Again the sideways glance followed by, "Yep, she does."

As Brad pulled up in front of the auto mechanic's shop, Chock expressed his thanks for giving him a lift. As he closed the door, he asked, "Mr. Miller, if you wouldn't mind, I'd like to have your permission to call on Sara May." After which he inhaled and simply held his breath.

"We have supper at five on Sundays, need to get a good night's rest for Monday. You can come for supper," said Brad.

"Okay," breathed Chock as he exhaled, "Sunday at five."

As was Chock's procedure, once he had engaged the services of a mechanic to retrieve his automobile and bring it to the shop for repairs, he rented a room for $10 per week and threw his suitcase into the closet for later unpacking. He left the boarding house and walked into the busy town, took a left at Main Street and soon was standing in front of the Sheriff's office. He entered and found the Sheriff sitting at his desk reviewing a written report.

"What can I do for you?" asked Ruell Pierce.

"Good afternoon," said Chock. "My name is Chock Dillard and I'm the assistant line manager for the Baltimore and Santa Fe Railroad." He advised the Sheriff that he was visiting Hendley to scout out possibilities of the railroad running an extension line into the area to help with transportation needs as the farmers and ranchers presently had only the unpaved roadway system to get their produce and cattle to market.

"About time," stated the Sheriff. He told Chock his name was Ruell Pierce and he was into his first term of office as Sheriff for the county. He also introduced his Deputy, Bud Leighton, who was in the process of cleaning three repeater Winchester rifles.

Ruell was a big man with a booming laugh and great physical strength. Everyone liked him as he was easygoing and easy to talk to. This trait was of great assistance when dealing with crime scene witnesses. He never met a stranger and was always the first to volunteer to help in times of need.

"This area could really grow with a rail line added," said Ruell.

"I always make it a priority to speak to the local law officer whenever I get to a new location. I figure he will best know what's going on in his town," Chock said.

"Well, he'd better or he won't be a sheriff for long," said Ruell. "How can we be of help?"

"I have a list of properties in which the railroad is interested in purchasing for the new line. We offer fair prices for land. Although the government can declare eminent domain and seize the properties outright, we have not done this and would hope not to. I would be thankful if you would look over the list of property owners whose land is being considered for purchase. If any of them cause a red flag warning, I'd rather know about it in advance, just to help avoid misunderstandings. Of course, this list is highly confidential and we would be very embarrassed if the wrong people got hold of it."

"Like you mean the newspaper, maybe? It would be pretty upsetting to learn your name and property were on some list being considered to be purchased or maybe even seized," replied Ruell.

After looking over the list, Ruell told Chock that none seemed to stand out. "When do you start?" he asked.

"Tomorrow morning, as soon as my car can be repaired. I bent a tie rod out near Brad Miller's place and it's being towed in to be repaired as we speak," said Chock.

"And how long do you suppose you'll be in town?" asked Ruell.

"Well, it could be some time as we are also looking to establish a field support office as a permanent part of the expansion. Hopefully, I will be able to be named the new District Superintendent when the support office is established," said Chock.

CHAPTER FOURTEEN

Hendley, Texas   *Spring 1905*

At 4:30 Sunday afternoon, Chock eased his car into the Miller's driveway and stopped at the side near the porch swing. The bouquet of flowers he held seemed awkward and heavy as he mounted the porch steps and knocked on the screen door.

Shortly, Sara May opened the door as he presented the flowers with a stutter, "Here, for you."

She smiled and accepted the flowers saying, "Wait here while I get something to put them in." She quickly returned with a vase and set it on the table in the front parlor, and placed the flowers inside. With a few deft movements, she quickly rearranged the flowers to her desire and said, "There, now don't these just look great – like a cool spring day."

Chock looked at the flowers again and it did seem as though they existed just to say, "Enjoy – we are pleased to make you feel happier." Before they had simply been a bouquet of flowers. Now, after Sara May's arrangement, they seemed different – better organized to show their colors and dependent on each other to exhibit their combined beauty. They were refreshing.

"Come on into the dining room, I just finished setting the table and Dad is coming in from his chores with the animals," Sara May said.

Her father entered the dining room from another door at the same time Chock entered from the parlor.

"Good afternoon, Mr. Miller," Chock said. "How are you today?"

"I'm fine and I'd really rather you just call me Brad like everyone else. Save that Mr. Miller business for matters of formality."

As they sat down at the table, Sara May came in from the kitchen with a large plate of fried chicken in one hand and a bowl of mashed potatoes in the other. The balance of the meal had already been placed on the table and the three sat down at the same time. Mr. Miller closed his eyes, placed the palms of his hands together before his face and began to pray. "Dear Heavenly Father, thank thee for thy bounty of good food and for the health of our loved ones – may you provide grace and understanding to we who are older as well as hope and happiness to those who are younger. Bless and keep safe our guest and may he be so inclined to return to this table again, he shall be welcome. Amen."

Chock sat still for a moment thinking about what Brad had said.

He looked at Sara May and saw her smile with a twinkle in her eye and then he relaxed. He had passed some sort of examination. He hoped his smile did not betray how thrilled he was to realize he had been given the okay not only to be there but to perhaps come again.

After the supper was finished, Sara May told her father to go out to the porch and enjoy his pipe. "We'll just be a few minutes with the dishes and then we'll have dessert."

Chock could hardly keep from smiling each time Sara handed him a plate to dry. She was happily telling about her plans to seek a teaching position at the local school. As she continued, Chock could hardly follow her conversation as each turn of her head seemed to present her beauty from a new angle. Suddenly, he realized she had stopped talking as she said, "Well, did you?"

"Did I what?"

"Decide to stay in town for a while?" she repeated. "You did say the railroad was looking to set up a new construction facility to oversee their expansion program didn't you?"

"Yes, oh yes, that is correct and I do believe this would be a great location for the office. I've looked at a couple of potential buildings and I'm sure we'll find one soon. I'll be staying for a while."

"How long will the expansion take?" she asked.

"Oh, probably a year or two depending on how difficult it will be to secure the rights of way."

"What an exciting time for you to be doing this. Bringing a whole new transportation system to an area to encourage development and commerce as well as improved passenger accommodation. Everyone gets so tired of having to travel the fifty miles to Bristow to catch the train now."

Chock finished the last dishes as Sara May untied her apron and moved the apple pie she had made onto the kitchen counter. She cut three ample pieces, placed them onto dessert plates and handed one to Chock.

"Let's join Dad on the porch to enjoy the evening breeze." She could just as easily have asked him to cross over the Sahara Desert and he would have agreed. Thankfully, the front porch held no such dramatic challenges.

Sara May stepped through the front door and handed a serving of pie to her father as she sat down in a porch chair. Chock sat down in the other chair and looked around to enjoy the sunset. The trees were still with no breeze and birds sang their evening tunes with careless abandon. As the trio on the porch finished their dessert, Chock asked Brad if he would object to him and Sara May taking a walk.

"Okay by me," Brad answered, "but she's the one who'll be doin' the walkin' so you better ask her," he said as he grinned through his puff of pipe smoke.

The dirt lane was dry from the rains and they chatted pleasantly as they strolled, enjoying the sunset filtering through the leaves and branches of the trees. Chock was totally infatuated and could not keep from smiling at each step of their walk. The lane was lined on each side with wild plum bushes which were all in bloom. The air smelled like perfume from the blossoms. Off in the distance, they heard the call of a whippoorwill.

"Wait," said Sara May as they stopped to listen. Again in the distance came the call "whippoorwill," "whippoorwill."

"See, that's his mate answering his call," she explained. They listened again as the two calls came somewhat closer together.

"Some people say they are Calling Birds, calling out to each other." The calls came again even closer than before. "See, they are finding each other," Sara May said as she smiled.

"And then what?" asked Chock.

"Why they do what birds do," said Sara May, at which Chock took her gently into his arms.

He then kissed her and said, "We are so fortunate to have found each other." Their kiss was long and passionate.

Spring 1906

Chock's car turned into the driveway at Brad Miller's house and he opened the door quickly. He stepped from the car and mounted the steps up onto the front porch, took a slow look all around, smiled to himself and knocked lightly on the screen door. Sara May opened the door saying, "Please come in, Chock."

"How are you today?" he asked.

"Just fine – never better."

"Is your father home?"

"He will be coming in from the fields shortly," she replied.

"How about I just walk out and meet him in the field? I have a very important question to pose to him and I really don't want to delay it," he said.

At that, Chock smiled brightly at Sara May and she returned his smile with one just as bright as his.

Chock saw Brad with his plow and team make a turn at the end of the large field behind the house and he headed toward him with a purpose in his gait. As he neared the team, Brad noticed Chock's approach, halted the team and rested the reins on the plow handles.

"Hey, Chock, what brings you out to the middle of this field on a warm day like today?"

"Well, sir, as you know, Sara May and I have been seeing each other two or three times a week for the past year and I must say she is the finest person I have ever met. Furthermore, I love her more than anything in the world and would like to have your permission to ask her to marry me."

"Well, I must say this doesn't exactly come as a surprise seeing how you two look at each other anytime you're together. And I agree she is a very fine person and will make you a great wife but you need to ask her. That would be fine by me," replied Brad. As he extended his hand, he said, "It'll be great to have you as my son-in-law."

Chock gripped the hard, calloused hand tightly and said, "I'll feel more like a son than you can imagine."

Chock walked quickly back to the house, called out to Sara May and asked if she would take a walk with him. She untied her apron, pushed at her hair and said, "It's a little warm to just take a walk but I'd go anywhere with you."

Chock beamed and held the door open for her. She stepped lightly out the door and down the steps with Chock close behind.

She skipped ahead a couple of steps, turned and asked, "Well, did you ask him?"

Chock feigned a puzzled look – "Ask him what? We just had a little chat about the weather and what not," he grinned.

"Speaking about weather never put a big smile on your face before so I think there's more to it than weather," said Sara May as she turned back toward the lane. The wild plum bushes were again in bloom. Chock quickly caught up to her and placed his hands on her sides and turned her to face him.

"Of course I asked your father if he would object to me marrying the most beautiful, loving young woman in the whole county. He said he had no problem with me marrying such a woman and did I have anyone specific in mind."

"He didn't say that, you spoof," said Sara May, and she made to slap him. At the last second, the slap turned into a caress of Chock's cheek. He held her hand and kissed it. He could no longer hold back his joy and he said, "I do have someone specific in mind. You know I love you more than life itself and want us to spend the rest of our lives together, so yes, will you please marry me?"

Sara May just said simply, "Yes, and I also love you more than life itself."

Their kiss was as long and passionate as their first kiss a year before when they had heard the calling birds call to each other.

CHAPTER FIFTEEN

Hendley, Texas   *Fall 1906*

C hock was nervously attempting to tie his tie when Ruell
Pierce said, "Here, give it to me. I know how to do it."

With that, Chock removed the tie and handed it to Ruell.
In turn, Ruell quickly tied the knot in the tie and slipped it over
Chock's head. Chock tightened the knot and took a quick look in
the mirror.

"That's fine – you'd think I had never tied a tie before," he
said, "but then again you don't get married all that often – just
nervous I guess."

"I was nervous on my wedding day," said Ruell, "but when I saw
my Mary coming down the aisle on her father's arm, everything just
seemed right and my nerves calmed down right then. She's had that
effect on me ever since."

Chock checked his watch – "Still more than an hour to go. I think I'll go downstairs to check on the decorations," he said.

"Be sure you don't peek in on Sara May – they say it brings bad luck if the groom sees his bride before she's being presented at the altar," said Ruell.

"No problem, besides, I think her bridesmaids and Maid of Honor would descend on me like a bunch of hornets if I even tried to get a peek," Chock said. "They've been here all morning helping her get dressed and made up."

"That's what women do," said Ruell. "My Mary spent most of yesterday getting herself dressed and undressed – this is the first time she has been a Maid of Honor."

"This wouldn't be a proper wedding if you weren't my Best Man and Mary wasn't Sara May's Maid of Honor," said Chock.

With that, he opened the door for Ruell to precede him down the stairs to the living room of Brad's house. Wedding decorations were gaily hung over the doors and windows. Balloons floated lazily near the ceiling. Chock grinned as he saw Brad putting the final decoration on a handmade altar at the end of the room.

"That looks real good – kind of formalizes the setting," said Chock to Brad.

"Well, she's been taking real good care of me – I'm going to miss her," said Brad.

"But we're not moving away, we'll be getting a place in town – no more than twenty minutes away."

"Now that brings up something else I've been meaning to speak to you about," Brad said. I'm getting too old to be farming and it's a lot of work to handle eighty acres. So I made a deal with my neighbor for him to purchase the land and I want you and Sara May to have this house as your wedding gift."

Chock was stunned. "But where are you going to live?"

"The money from the sale of the land has provided enough to purchase a home in town and income for me to live on," Brad said. "My needs are simple and it doesn't take much to keep me going."

Chock looked around the room and shook his head as if to say, "This is too much. Gaining a wife and a home all in the same day."

Ruell extended his hand to Chock and said, "Congratulations, homeowner, taxpayer, handyman and all the other responsibilities that come with owning a home."

Chock shook his hand and then went out onto the porch to sit in the swing. The breeze was cool and it was quite relaxing. Chock felt a swelling of pride as he realized the trust and faith Brad had bestowed upon him. He knew he would do all that was possible to maintain that trust and faith. With Sara May at his side, he felt all things could be possible.

Shortly, Ruell came to the door and said, "It's time to start," at which Chock practically leaped from the swing.

"I'm ready," he said as he opened the screen and entered the house. He and Ruell took their places near the altar. The room was filled with friends and relatives all abuzz with anticipation as the pianist began playing the wedding march.

Sara May and her father began descending the stairway with her right arm around her father's left. Chock almost gasped as he took in her radiance and beauty. Her gown was as though it had been molded to her figure and her hair was up in a swirl around her head. Her veil was very thin and only barely hid her face.

They reached the bottom of the stairs and turned to face Chock and Ruell. The minister stepped up to the altar as Sara May and Brad moved through the crowd toward them. A few steps before reaching Chock, they stopped. Brad lifted the veil from his daughter's face, gave her a light kiss and said, "I love you," at which he replaced the veil and turned to place Sara May's hand into Chock's extended hand.

The minister began, "Dearly beloved, we are gathered together to . . ."

Chock kept glancing sideways to see Sara May's calm, glowing smile and each time he smiled as well. The minister was directing his attention to Chock. "Do you take this woman to be your wife . . .?" and then to Sara May, "Do you take this man to be your husband . . .?" Then he was asking for the ring which Ruell produced and handed to him. "This ring symbolizes . . ." and before Chock knew it, he was saying, "Now you may kiss the bride," and as they kissed, the minister stated, "Ladies and gentlemen, may I present to you Mr. and Mrs. Chock Dillard."

The room erupted in applause.

CHAPTER SIXTEEN

M iss Kathy May looked on disapprovingly as Ken retrieved his power lawn mower and edging tools from the storage shed near her garage. He occasionally mowed her lawn in exchange for her letting him store his mower and tools in her shed. The mower had been purchased on credit from Bryman's Hardware. Ten dollars down and $5 a week until it was paid off. Ken paid it off early.

"Why do you want to play that old football?" she asked again. It had been a topic of disagreement between them ever since they became friends three years before. "You're just going to get something broken or maimed for life, and for what? To run up and down some field carrying a ball? It doesn't make sense to me."

Ken sighed and said, "I know you worry, but I'm pretty big and fast for my age – the coach thinks I might have a chance for a scholarship to college if I continue to improve. That may be my best chance to get a real education."

Kathy May drew in her breath with a loud choke. "You mean you want to play this football on into college?" she asked with true concern in her voice. "Those college boys are much bigger and stronger – you're sure to get hurt."

Again Ken sighed and said, "That will be three years from now. I'll be a lot bigger and stronger too."

Shaking her head in disbelief, she called Ken to her and said, "Most people don't know it but I receive a fairly substantial income from oil wells drilled by my poppa when he was a young man. There are no restrictions on how I choose to use that money. I could afford to pay your way through college if you would just give up your notion to play football. This would allow you to devote your full efforts to doing well with your studies."

"That's very generous of you, but you need to understand that I actually enjoy playing the game and my coaches tell me I am good at it. I also don't believe it will detract me from earning good grades in my classes," responded Ken.

He was truly touched by the offer just made by Miss Kathy May but he knew he would not feel proper in accepting her offer. He needed to retain his feeling of independence.

Miss Kathy May responded, "Just keep my offer in your thoughts should you change your mind. Also, please do not reveal that I receive this special income. If people knew about it, I would probably have a crowd at my doorstep every morning looking for a handout. You can take my word that the money is used for good purposes and for the benefit of others."

"Don't worry, Miss Kathy May, your secret is safe with me and I won't ever discuss this conversation with anyone else," said Ken.

During the years, she and Ken had become very good friends. She almost felt he had become her son as she had never married and had no known relatives. She marveled at his growing maturity and truly felt a love like a mother for him. Ken treasured her friendship as well, as his relationship with his own family seemed to be growing further apart rather than together. His father spent a greater amount of time with his business and less and less time with his family. They all seemed to be going in different directions and their time spent together was less than ever before. No one seemed to really care how the family was disintegrating right before their eyes. His mother seemed to be just going through the motions and not really engaged in holding the family close. Meanwhile, it seemed to Ken that Miss Kathy May held her relationship with him closer and closer. She never failed to ask how his education was progressing. She frequently loaned him books from her substantial library and was always available for discussion and advice if he asked her for it. She had shared some of her life experiences but always tried to keep them on a positive note. Ken was most fond of the story about how her mother and father had fallen in love strolling down a pleasant country lane while listening to the calling birds call to each other.

CHAPTER SEVENTEEN

Hendley, Texas   *Spring 1914*

Kathy May's father and Ruell B. Pierce were best friends. They became acquainted when her father first came to look for land for the railroad. By accident, Kathy May caused Ruell's name to be changed.

Chock, Kathy May and her brother Jackie were in town at the mercantile store putting in a replenishment of store purchases and supplies. Just as they came out of the store, Ruell Pierce was coming down the sidewalk with an entourage carrying signs that said, "Vote for Pierce," "Pierce for Sheriff" and "Re-Elect Pierce." Chock, Kathy May and Jackie were all just a few feet from Ruell when he stuck out his hand to Chock and said, "Good to see you Chock." Kathy May's poppa replied that he was proud to vote for him and would be of any assistance.

Ruell then turned to Kathy May and said, "Hi there, little girl, what's your name?" knowing full well that she was Chock Dillard's daughter.

"Kathy May," she replied.

Ruell let out a big laugh, leaned over and picked Kathy May up, and placed her on the back of a flatbed truck parked next to the sidewalk. Ruell was married with no children, in fact, he and his wife were never able to have children. Ruell absolutely loved children – and everyone, children included, liked Ruell. He turned to the crowd with a quieting motion of his hands as if to say, "Now everyone listen up, this is gonna be good." He gave Kathy May a serious look and said, "Now my name's Ruell Pierce and I'm running for re-election for Sheriff. Now who are you gonna vote for?" knowing full well that women were not yet allowed to vote. Ruell could not possibly have known that at that time in her life, she had a slight speech impediment and it was difficult for her to say words with the letter R in them. At any rate, Kathy May sang out in a loud voice "Ruell Pierce" only it didn't come out as Ruell Pierce but more like "Bull Piss." The crowd roared while Ruell stood before her with a look of shock and surprise on his face like she had never seen before. The crowd began to chant, "We want Bull, we want Bull." Ruell's face changed with a slow, broad smile and he turned to the crowd and said, "You want Bull?" at which the crowd roared their enthusiastic approval. Ruell was a natural politician and he sensed he had just found a gem.

"All right," he yelled, "you want Bull, you got Bull." And from that day on he was known as Bull Pierce. When not in his presence, many people called him Bull Piss but that just endeared him to them even more. The local newspaper played the story out and it spread rapidly. Everyone would say, "Are you voting for Bull Piss or the other guy?" Everyone seemed to forget about the other guy and Bull won in a landslide. He was truly one of the best men Kathy May had ever known.

Poppa was known as a smart, clear thinker with no vices although he did like to participate in an occasional card game in one of the numerous local gambling halls. In his early days on the railroad, he may have had his share of "vices of the body" but he never talked about them. Kathy May always suspicioned he had advanced not just because he was smart but because he also could present a good side to just about any situation. He always said, "If you really stop and analyze the problem, you will see the answer since the problem contains the answer. You just have to know how to look for it."

More than a few times, Kathy May would stomp away from Chock after having asked for an answer to some problem in her schoolwork. He would always coax her back and work to show her how to solve the problem. He never gave her the answers, just coached her in how to really look at a problem, break it down into each of its smallest components and reach an understanding of how all the parts fit together. When doing so, the answer generally became obvious and she was surprised to have not seen it earlier. Chock had that rare gift of being able to see twice as much as ordinary people. Really successful police detectives and investigators have that gift as well.

CHAPTER EIGHTEEN

Hendley, Texas   *Summer 1919*

C hock looked at the cards. Three kings and two eights. The best hand he had seen in two hours. The other four men at the table all stared at their hands. Toby Babson dropped two chips into the pile in the center of the table and advised he would open for $20. Jake Jenks, sitting next to him, laughed and said, "Hell, that ain't no bet, that's an apology," and dropped $50 into the pot. "Now, that's a bet!" he announced with a swagger in his voice. Bill Thompson sat next to Jake and said this was too rich for his blood and threw his cards onto the pile of chips. Chock checked his pile of chips, carefully picked up a stack and quietly announced, "There's your $50 plus $50 more." Jake almost bit his cigar in half but said nothing. Carl Abner, sitting between Chock and Toby, took a full minute before slowly dropping his cards onto the pile when announcing, "I just don't think my little pair justifies that big of a bet."

Toby had taken everything in and dropped in his chips with a soft, "Call."

Everyone turned to look at Jake, who had begun to sweat profusely. His week's growth of beard gave him an ominous appearance. "Now ain't that sweet," he snarled. "Got two of you boys left to see how good my cards are. Well, not just yet, it's gonna cost you to see them," he growled, as he dropped a large handful of chips into the pile. "There's your $50 plus $100 more."

Chock looked at his cards and calmly announced, "Call," as he dropped another stack of chips onto the pile. From all outward appearances, Chock seemed totally relaxed. Inside his heart was racing like crazy. Yes, he had played poker lots of times but never for the kind of stakes now sitting on the table. He estimated the pile of chips was worth nearly $700. Chock had never played for that kind of money in his life.

"Not for me," announced Toby as he dropped his cards onto the table.

"Well, read 'em and weep," snarled Jake as he spread out the two queens and two nines onto the table and reached for the pile of chips.

"I'm reading but I'm not weeping," said Chock, as he laid the three kings and two eights on top of the pile.

The veins in Jake's neck and forehead throbbed as he looked at Chock. With a look of disbelief, he sat back in his chair.

Chock began pulling the pile toward his side of the table.

"Hold it," snapped Jake, "I'm not done yet." He pulled a folded paper from his coat pocket. "This here is the bill of sale for the

Jenks' Drilling Company. I was on my way to meet Bill Bradley this evening to sell my drilling company to him. He said he would give me $2,000 for it." With that, he slapped the paper down onto the pile of chips. "Just you and me Dillard, no one else. One hand of five card draw with winner takes all, no betting, no raises, nothing but just that pile of chips against my drilling company," said Jake.

Chock slowly slid the pile of chips back to the center of the table. "Alright Jake, just you and me, but Abner deals the cards."

The room had grown completely quiet as everyone in the gambling hall had stopped whatever they were doing to watch what was going on. Abner gathered the cards and began to shuffle quickly. He set the deck onto the table and turned to Chock and said, "Cut 'em."

Chock picked off about a third of the deck and set them down onto the table toward Abner. Abner picked up the cards and began to deal. Back and forth between Jake and Chock until each man had five cards before him.

"Okay, pick 'em up," said Abner. Jake jerked the cards off the table and held them below the table, close to his belly and eyed the cards carefully.

Chock picked up his cards, leaned back and slowly fanned them out – one at a time – two threes with a seven, a nine and a jack. "Discards," instructed Abner.

"I'll take three," Jake snarled as he dropped his three discards onto the stack.

"Give me three too," said Chock as he dropped his discards onto the table.

Again Jake grabbed his new cards and leaned back. His face went from a scowl to a smile as he looked at the cards. "Well, well, well," he said. "Just looky here," as he laid out the two sixes, two queens and an eight. "Let's see you beat two pair," he snarled.

Chock had not yet even looked at his new cards. He set the pair of threes down onto the pile and turned over the first card of his new draw – a jack. Chock winced thinking of the jack he had just moments before discarded. He slowly turned over his second card – a ten – and taking a deep breath, he slowly turned over his last card, the three of spades. "Three threes" someone yelled. "Chock wins," yelled someone else. Chock was too drained to even take note when Jake jumped out of his chair and yelled, "You cheated! I don't know how but you cheated me out of my company."

Abner said, "No he didn't, I dealt the cards, there wasn't any way Chock could have cheated. This just isn't your day, Jake."

"Not my day, not my day," yelled Jake, as he pulled a pistol from his coat pocket. With it pointed straight at Chock, he said, "If this just ain't my day, then neither is it yours."

Time stopped, Jake's face was pulled into a grimace and his cheek began to jerk. No one moved.

"I'll see you in hell," screamed Jake at Chock, then he quickly stuck the pistol into his own mouth and pulled the trigger. Blood and brains sprayed onto the wall behind Jake as chaos broke loose in the room. Some screamed, some ran, some dived for the floor. Chock sat in stunned silence watching the commotion around him. He picked up the Bill of Sale for the drilling company and began to pull the pile of chips slowly toward himself.

The next morning Chock drove out to the drilling site where the Jenks' Drilling rig was set up. As he drew up in front of the rig, four sets of eyes centered on him with suspicion.

"Morning," said Chock. "I'm Chock Dillard and I kind of own this rig now."

"So we heard," responded the little red-headed Irishman. "Jenks was a cruel, hard-pushing son of a bitch and never gave a damn about us or anything else. What kind of a son of a bitch are you?"

Chock laughed and said, "Most people don't think I'm a son of a bitch. That's a title I work hard to avoid. I expect a fair day's work for a fair day's pay. If that idea appeals to you and the rest of the crew, you're welcome to stay on. Otherwise, you'd best be moving on."

The little Irishman stared at Chock and then finally said, "I guess it takes someone with a lot of guts to offer to fire an entire crew at first sight."

"That's not what I said. I said I expect a fair day's work for a fair day's pay and if that wasn't okay by you and the crew, you'd best be moving on. If you choose to leave, I'd say you would be quitting, not being fired," said Chock.

The little Irishman said, "Son of a bitch, not only does he have guts, he's got a brain too. Well guys, what do you say?"

"I ain't never quit a job before and I ain't startin' today," said the black man standing next to the little Irishman. He stuck out his hand toward Chock and said, "Pleased to meet you, Mr. Chock. My name's Collin Jones and I been working on this drilling rig for four years. I'd be mighty pleased to keep on stayin' on."

Chock shook his hand and said to the big Indian at the tail end of the drilling rig, "How about you – are you staying or leaving?"

"Me stay, run drill rig," said the big Indian.

"And what's your name?" asked Chock.

"My name Lahontan but most everyone call me Chief," advised the big Indian.

"How about you?" asked Chock as he addressed the thin, short man standing next to the Indian.

"Seeing how I don't have any other opportunities available, guess I'll just stay on with you. You gonna meet the payroll on Friday?" asked the thin man.

"Of course I will," said Chock. "What's your name?"

"Ben Crenshaw," he replied.

"I knew a man named Ben when I was first starting out with the railroad," said Chock. "He was one of the smartest men I ever knew. He could get a crew going by just telling a story and always ending it with a smile."

"Sounds like a good guy to know," said Ben with a big smile.

"I think I like you already," said Chock.

Chock looked back to the little Irishman and said, "I sure could use an experienced tool pusher. Any idea where I might find one?"

"You're looking at the best in the business and I ain't leavin' either. Name's Sean McCoy but everyone just calls me Red."

"Sounds good to me," said Chock.

There had been times when drilling was slow and other periods when no work was available. During those times they just hunkered down and took odd jobs to stay afloat.

Recently, a couple of other drilling crews had come into the area and rumor had it that they were going to try to drill for oil. When Chock mentioned this to the crew, Sean said, "You should talk to Chief. He has said his father used to get oil from a sump out on the prairie."

When Chock approached Lahontan and asked if he knew about oil, he told Chock that he should speak to his father as he knew about oil from the old days. Chock asked him if he would take him to meet with his father and discuss what he knew about oil. Lahontan said he would – that his father lived across the Red River in Oklahoma – not too far, maybe two hours by auto. Chock asked when they could go and the big Indian said, "Anytime, he will be there."

"How can you be sure of that?" Chock asked.

"He got no other place to go so he will be there."

"Well, let's go right now, time's a wasting," said Chock.

Chock and Lahontan drove north and soon crossed the Red River by ferry into Oklahoma, which only a few years earlier was known as Indian Territory where many tribes had been relocated from their ancestral homes in the Eastern and Northern States. Many thousands had died during this period of relocation, aptly named the Trail of Tears. Eventually, the government set up a program to allot each Indian a parcel of land consisting of 160 acres, or one-fourth of a square mile. Tribal land left unallotted to the Indians was purchased by the government for a few cents per acre. This land was then opened for settlement by whites, and thus began the famous land rush. Some of the white settlers snuck onto sites in the territory before the official rush day and became known as sooners. (The name was later adopted by the University of Oklahoma to call their student body.) In 1907, the area had been admitted to the Union as the forty-sixth state with the name of Oklahoma. The 160-acre allotment would theoretically provide sufficient land for an Indian to farm and be self-sufficient. In actuality, much of the land was of poor quality and unsuitable to be successfully farmed. At other times, drought, freezing winters and grasshoppers would destroy the crops and the Indians suffered greatly. Some sold their land for cheap to unscrupulous whites and others were simply cheated out of their allotments.

Chock and Lahontan rode down the dirt road through rows of corn and occasionally an area covered with melons. Lahontan's family had been one of the fortunate ones and their land was rich and productive. The pair pulled up in front of a somewhat ramshackle house with an old battered car parked in front. "He's here. That's his car," said Lahontan. He knocked on the door and spoke in his native tongue to the man who answered.

Lahontan introduced Chock to his father, Pitchlynn Running Bear. Lahontan said that his father had been chief of their tribe over the years, but most of the Indians had drifted away as there was no way for them to make a living. Lahontan's father advised Chock that he still owned his land allotment as well as Lahontan's mother's, plus Lahontan's. Altogether, there were 480 acres on which his home was now located. They farmed a portion of the land in corn, and eked by with help from the local Indian agent who dispersed a limited amount of government commodities and supplies.

Chock asked if Lahontan's father had ever seen oil on the land, and he replied that yes, there was a sump where sometimes a tar-like substance collected on the surface, and they used it to rub onto their joints believing it would help with the pain. Asked if it worked, he said, "Sometimes yes, sometimes no." The Indians did not believe oil as they knew it had any real value. The smoke generated by burning was so black, it could not be used for cooking or heating their lodges and teepees. They did sometimes use it for torches but it was considered a nuisance by most.

Chock asked if there were any oil slicks on their land, and the answer was no. He told Chock that there were some areas of the land where there were bad smells coming from the earth, which they called the Land of Stinks, and that sometimes the Indians had lit the bad air coming from the ground and it would burn continuously until they would smother it out.

Chock asked if Running Bear could take him to the Land of Stinks and see if they could drill for oil there. He said that if they found oil, they would sell it and split the profits fifty/fifty: half for him who owned the land and half for Chock for drilling for it. They agreed and Chock advised he would bring his drilling rig and crew the following day for Running Bear to direct them to a likely spot.

The following day, Chock drove his crew and rig to Lahontan's father's place and at his direction, they began maneuvering his rig across the terrain. It was tough going as there were no roads and numerous obstacles to overcome: deer trails and scrub brush with areas heavily wooded with black-jack and post oak trees. Finally,

Running Bear indicated an area near a dry stream bed where it proved very difficult to maneuver the drill rig into place. Eventually, with a lot of sweat and strain, the crew had the rig in place and Chock asked, "Are you sure this is the right place?" Running Bear simply stood with his arms folded with no response.

Chock was tired, sweaty and generally beat from moving the rig into such a remote location, and he said, "That's it? You have us drag this unit all over the place, set it up in this hell for what place and now just stand there with your arms folded not saying a word?"

All the while, Running Bear did not speak.

"Hell, there's nothing here but rattlesnakes and jackrabbits," said Chock.

"Oil everywhere," said Running Bear.

"Oil everywhere?" said Chock. "Then why did you have us drag this drilling unit all over to hell and gone?"

At which Running Bear spread his arms wide and said again, "Oil everywhere."

Chock stared and said, "Oil everywhere?" at which he laughed and looked all around saying, "Oil everywhere again and again. Oil everywhere! I'll be damned."

After a week of drilling, they still had not hit anything. "Keep going," Chock directed his crew.

Chock wiped sweat from his brow. The crew had taken a break from their drilling efforts to catch a few minutes of rest in the shade of the drilling rig.

Each took a few swallows of water from the water bucket as the ladle was passed around.

"Well, what do you think, Sean?" asked Chock.

"I don't know anything about finding oil, just hard drilling," Sean replied. "I figure we're down about 800 feet so we'll just keep punching until something comes up."

The crew restarted the drilling rig, rising and dropping, rising and dropping. All of a sudden, they stopped. "Did you hear something?" asked Sean. "Yeah, like something just growled." At that, a geyser of oil sprang from the drill hole and began spraying the ground around them. They were all jumping and slapping each other's hands in joy. "Get the spud head in place," yelled Chock. "Get this thing capped off so we can control it and stop wasting this black gold."

The crew was eventually able to get the well capped and Chock instructed them to begin the process of moving the rig to a new drill location. He would go into town and make arrangements to have oil storage tanks set up at the site and to contract for trucks to transport the oil to the refinery.

Thus began the history of the Dillard Drilling Company and later the Dillard Production and Transportation Company. Eventually, the company developed well over 300 producing wells. The proceeds made Chock wealthy as well as numerous landowners, primarily Native Americans.

Chock always treated the Indians fairly and never tried to steal any of their share of money from the drilling successes. When he hit a dry hole, Chock simply shook the landowner's hand, apologized and moved his rig to a new location to try again. The Indians trusted him and recommended to their fellow landowners to allow Chock to drill. He would always treat them with respect and honesty. Many of them became wealthy and assisted their fellow tribesmen in getting to enjoy a better life.

CHAPTER NINETEEN

Hendley, Texas   *Spring 1958*

Ken smiled to himself as he strode up the walk toward Miss Kathy May's front door. The pecan trees still stood tall and provided welcome shade on a warm day. Yes, they would produce another bumper crop of nuts that would fall and the crows and squirrels would have a great time since Ken would not be available to harvest them as he had done the previous five years.

The large knocker made its usual announcement of his arrival and soon the door opened. Miss Kathy May smiled and said, "What a nice occasion to see you again." Ken always felt somewhat self-conscious sitting in the parlor as Miss Kathy May prepared the usual tea service. When everything was in place and she had poured the tea and mixed the sugar and lemon, she said, "Now tell me, what is this exciting news you have to share?"

"My scholarship came through – you know, the football scholarship to play for Mid-Central State at Amarillo."

"Oh, that again. I had hoped it would not happen as I so fear you will be badly hurt. It is such a rough game. Are you sure this is the best thing for you?"

"Yes, I'm sure," said Ken, "and it allows me to major in political science as I hope to someday become a lawyer. This is a really great opportunity and I actually love the game of football."

Kathy May was thinking back to her past. "I just fear the thought of losing you. I lost my brother when I was young and life has never been the same since. I think about him every day."

Rural Oklahoma   *Spring 1921*

Kathy May and her brother Jackie were in the back seat of Chock's Model T as it bounced along the rough road. Chock was on his way to check on the progress of one of his drilling rigs. It was Saturday and Kathy May and Jackie were along for the adventure. They had never been to a drill site with their father before, so the day held the promise of new experiences.

Chock pulled up near where the drilling rig was operating. He cautioned Kathy May and Jackie to take a look around but to keep back from the actual work area. He wouldn't be long and then they could continue their trip to town to purchase supplies.

Recent spring rains had swollen the nearby river to the top of its banks. Kathy May and Jackie tossed a ball back and forth, all the while drifting generally in the direction of the river. Kathy May heaved the ball toward Jackie but he missed it and it bounced into the water.

"Don't worry," Jackie said, "I can get it." At which he kicked off his shoes, rolled up the pants of his overalls and strode into the river. The current picked up the ball and Jackie moved farther out in his effort to get to the ball.

"Jackie, be careful!" yelled Kathy May. Her shout carried back to the drill rig where Collin Jones turned to look just as Jackie slipped and was pulled in by the current. Collin dropped his tools and sprinted toward the river just in time to see a broken tree being swept downstream. Jackie was struggling mightily as a branch of the tree caught one of his overall straps and pulled him under the water. Collin reached the edge of the river and dived in. The tree was downstream about ten yards and gaining speed as it was now turned sideways to the current, dragging Jackie farther down. Kathy May was screaming and yelling as Chock reached her side. The tree was now out of sight around a bend in the river. Collin stumbled onto the side of the river and fell to his knees. He sobbed, "I'm sorry, Mr. Chock, I'm sorry. I had him by his foot but the current was too strong and he was pulled out of my hand. I couldn't catch up again and now he's gone." At that Collin collapsed to the ground and choked out his sobs.

Chock hugged Kathy May and tried to calm her down but she could not be consoled. Chock, himself, was so much in shock he could hardly speak. Finally, he said to Collin to get the truck and follow him. There was a bridge over the river about a mile downstream. They would go there and see if they could spot the tree holding Jackie down.

They got to the bridge and after a few minutes, they saw the tree. The river was wider at this point and the current was moving more slowly.

Collin and Chock waded into the river and were able to grab the tree and move it to the bank. It was there where Chock was able to pull Jackie's lifeless body loose from the tree branches. He laid his son on the ground and began to pump hard on his back in an effort to revive him. After fifteen minutes he was exhausted and after no response from Jackie, he had to accept the fact that Jackie was gone.

Kathy May was devastated. She felt it was all her fault as she had thrown the ball that went into the river. Over and over again she replayed their game of catch, trying to will a different ending. She could only cry at night. Chock just sat and stared. Even after Jackie's funeral, he and Sara May just went through the motions of living. Even frequent visits by Bull Pierce did nothing to relieve the grief felt through the entire house.

Eventually, Kathy May was able to return to school. Chock resumed running his drilling company but hardly ever smiled. Sara May was the one who took the longest to return to some degree of normalcy. She would sometimes carry on a conversation with her son as though he still lived. Slowly, she recovered from her grief, but inside she still suffered.

CHAPTER TWENTY

Amarillo, Texas   *Fall 1962*

T he crowd was large and boisterous as Ken and Billy Don
worked their way toward their group of friends at the back of
the Lucky Doggers – the local hangout for their teammates and the
scene of historic beer consumption on nights before and after big
games. It was slow going as everyone they encountered yelled the
same question above the hubbub and din of the crowd.

"Hey, Billy Don, who's gonna win tomorrow?"

"We are," yelled Billy Don in response, holding his right arm in
the air with the classic clinched fist signal.

"And just how do you know?" the crowd inquired.

"Because I, by God, say so," yelled back Billy Don.

The interchange had become part of the ritual and Billy Don
had been right eighteen out of the twenty times he had been the
starting quarterback for Mid-Central State University. It was

just another part of his larger-than-life image. He was big, tall, handsome and a gifted athlete, and these qualities had shaped him and his image into something bigger than life. People naturally gravitated to him and he was pretty much the center of attention no matter where he went.

Ken grinned as the pretty young coed asked if he could introduce her to Billy Don. "Sure, how about 2:30 next Tuesday afternoon?" asked Ken. Her crestfallen look caused Ken to stop and say he was sorry he had made such a flip remark but it was just that about fifty other coeds had asked the same question in the last week. "Why would you want to be number fifty-one?" he asked her.

"It wouldn't matter if I was number 151," responded the coed, "it would be worth it just to get to meet him."

Ken had seen this type of hero worship and adulation before. He wasn't sure he understood it but that didn't change the fact that Billy Don exerted some sort of power over normal people. Maybe it was the way he could make everyone in the room feel like they had known him personally even though they had only met ten minutes earlier.

Women especially seemed mesmerized by this gift and Billy Don never failed to have numerous romantic opportunities available at any given moment in time.

Ken and Billy Don had been roommates and teammates since their first day at Mid-Central State University in 1958. Ken was well aware of the long hours of study and reading Billy Don worked into his schedule. Many people were not even aware of the 3.8 GPA he maintained as a Political Science major, second on the football squad only to Ken's own 3.9. They often bantered with each other in private about who had the highest IQ, but never in public. Over the four years they had been roommates, no serious arguments had ever developed. Ken recognized Billy Don for the natural leadership he possessed just as Billy Don appreciated Ken for his high degree of intelligence and compassion. He often called Ken the most compassionate, butt-kicking, ball-catching athlete to ever walk the face of the earth.

For his part, Ken realized his ability to catch Billy Don's passes on the gridiron came not only from his own athletic capabilities but also from an inane ability they possessed to communicate the needs and flow of the game to each other. Billy Don called it the zip and said when the zip flowed, everything seemed like it was aligned and flowing. Ken sensed the feel and flow between the two of them. They connected on a different level than the other players.

When a play was broken or Billy Don was in trouble, through some sort of sixth sense, Ken would just know where he needed to be, and through another sense, Billy Don knew just where and how hard to throw the football. He didn't even need to see Ken, he just knew he would be there. On numerous occasions, the sports announcers and game analysts had commented that these two seemed to be connected by some sort of invisible wire, unseen by others but in some way providing the connection that allowed each to sense the other's place occupied in the game. Ken realized he could never experience the success of play on the field with anyone else at quarterback. On the few occasions in his career when someone else had to run the offense for a part of the game, he had been simply another member of the team, going through his routes and blocking assignments, no more outstanding or noteworthy than any other modestly talented wide receiver.

As they reached the group of athletes at the rear of the club, a cheer went up – "B.D., B.D., B.D." Holding both hands above his head, Billy Don gazed at the ceiling and said, "Oh, Lord, you are munificent in your blessing," at which the group roared and yelled, "How many? How many?"

Billy Don yelled back, "Nuff for Tuff, Nuff for Tuff." Meaning the team would score enough touchdowns the next day to satisfy head coach Howard Tuffington, affectionately called Coach "Tuff" by his staff and players. This entire scenario was all part of the ritual developed over the career of Billy Don Preston, recognized as one of the finest quality quarterbacks to come through the University in the past twenty years. As Billy Don drank down a large glass of beer, a large man in the crowd snapped a picture, at which one of the offensive linemen bumped him rather soundly, causing the man to drop his camera. As he bent to pick it up, another bump sent him sprawling across the floor while his camera simply disappeared into the group of players. As the man was being helped to his feet, the huge lineman was profuse in his apologies, "Sorry, man, someone bumped me into you."

"Yeah, yeah, okay, where's my goddamned camera?"

Another of the linemen held the camera out – the roll of exposed film trailing like a limp kite's tail. "Aw, gee, looks like it must have popped open when you dropped it," said the football player.

The man's face reddened as he allowed how it had never "popped open" before. "Well, y'all have fun at the game tomorrow," said the lineman as he patted the man with a resounding back slap. The man staggered forward and just managed to hold onto the roll of exposed film in time to keep from dropping the camera again. "Shit" he yelled to no one in particular. "I had a great shot of Billy Don chuggin' a cold one."

The man next to him said, "Don't you know it's considered bad luck to try to get a shot of Billy Don doing something he may not be too proud of someday? Especially on the eve of the last big game in his career? That could almost be un-American let alone plain dumb with this club full of Billy Don's friends and fellow players. You're lucky just the film got exposed. At least they gave your camera back."

A slow look of realization spread over the man's face as he comprehended what the fan had said. "Yeah, well that don't mean Billy Don didn't do it anyway."

"Says who?" said the man with the glasses. "I didn't see him do anything wrong," he leered toward the man.

The next afternoon the sun was bright and toward the end of the fourth quarter of the ball game, the score was tied fourteen to fourteen. The team was huddled in the center of the field as Billy Don was calling the play.

"Okay guys, here we go – twenty-eight fly, forty-seven left on two." This play called for Ken to flank to the right before sprinting at all-out speed straight down the field while the tight end flared to the left side of the field. The defensive team had lined up with five linemen, four linebackers and two cornerbacks.

At these times, Ken could hear the old song in his head – "And the circle won't be broken, by and by Lord, by and by." Billy Don asked, "Ken, are you hearing it? Are you hearing it?"

"For sure," replied Ken, as the huddle broke and the team lined up at the line of scrimmage. The ball was snapped to Billy Don and he dropped back, faked a throw to his left toward the flaring tight end then turned and let the football fly toward a spot deep down the field in Ken's direction. The deception had worked perfectly. The deep defender on the left side had collapsed in to help defend the faked pass to the tight end, leaving only the right side defender available to defend his area. By the time he realized the true nature of the play, Ken was already past him.

"Poppa sang bass, Mama sang tenor . . ." the song played in his head. One look over his left shoulder and he could see the pass high in the air and true on course. At the last second with the song playing out he could hear, "In the sky, Lord, in the sky" – as he leaped as far as he could and felt the ball land in his outstretched hands. The defender hurled his body into Ken but too late, the ball was caught, Ken was in the end zone and the referee was signaling a touchdown. The last catch of Ken's football career to win the game.

CHAPTER TWENTY-ONE

Rural Hendley, Texas   *Summer 1922*

C ollin Jones eased himself back into the wood porch swing and chuckled as he watched his son and daughter chase fireflies in the early dusk. The tiredness fell slowly from his shoulders but it was a good tiredness. The kind that came from hard, honest work. That seemed to Collin to be the only kind he had ever known – hard work and the honest part as well. He had grown up with six brothers and three sisters at a time when everyone had to scramble to keep body and soul together. His mother and father were uneducated field hands but had subscribed to a belief in the almighty, and hard work. Two of his brothers had left at an early age to seek their fortunes elsewhere. The grip of the land was not strong on them like it had been on Collin. Somehow, he knew his brothers' chase of the good life would come to no good, and sure enough, his oldest brother had been killed in a gang fight and the other was in prison near Chicago. Collin was not sure of all the details, just that his brother had been in the wrong place at the wrong time. Three other brothers were scattered over the southern area of the state and maintained an occasional correspondence. The three sisters had all married young and had various quantities of children to raise. Again, he did not hear from them often – only when trouble visited their lives and they needed help. The youngest of the family, Clayton, at thirteen, had come to live with Collin and his family after both parents died in the great flu epidemic the previous winter.

He called out to his wife, Carrie, to ask if there was any lemonade left from the supper meal. She leaned against the doorway framed by the light of the kerosene lamp in their three-room shack and allowed how there was just enough for two more cupfuls.

"Well, dog my hide," laughed Collin. "Sure would be nice for you and me to have those two cups."

She brought the lemonade and sat next to him and they sipped it quietly, keeping an eye on the children now poking at a toad hopping in her flower bed.

Three sets of headlights bounced as they turned onto the lane from the main road a quarter mile away. Collin frowned since no one they knew was expected at this time of night. Intuitively, he knew something was wrong.

"Get the children in the house," he instructed his wife.

She called them and then again. They sensed a tone of fear in her voice as they dropped their play and bounced up the steps, over the porch and into the shack just as the first of the three cars pulled up to a stop thirty feet in front of their shack. White-robed men began to disgorge from the cars, all with full hoods and robes. Collin stood and asked, "What y'all doin' here?"

"Just came to have a little chat," came a voice from behind the mask. "We think it's about time you moved on – gettin' a little high and mighty with that Chock Dillard fellow. It ain't right that some nigger gets a drilling job when there's plenty of white boys looking for work."

"Ain't no reason to be upset at me. Mr. Jenks done hired me years ago and trained me on the drillin' machine. I worked for half pay for the first year so I could learn."

"All that don't matter no how," snarled one of the masks. "We're givin' you till Saturday to clear out or we're gonna string you up. We'll be back Saturday night. Either we'll burn you out or string you up – the choice is yours."

One of the hooded men threw a lighted torch onto the porch. Collin kicked at it and stomped the flames out while the three cars motored back to the main road.

Collin's wife came behind and grabbed onto him so tight he could scarcely breathe. Her trembling was severe and she could barely speak. "What we gonna do?" she asked with tears streaming down her face. "We got no place to go – this is the only home we've ever known."

"I know, I know," said Collin. "I'll talk to Mr. Chock tomorrow and see if he can do anything."

"You heard them," said his wife. "They blame you for having a job with him. What can he do?"

"I don't know, I just don't know."

The next morning Collin approached Chock at the drill site. "Mr. Chock, I gots to leave, I gots to leave right away."

"Well now, just a minute," said Chock. "What's happened? You weren't like this yesterday. Besides, where could I get a trained swamper to take your place?"

"It don't matter no how, Mr. Chock. I gots to leave. The Klan done paid us a visit last night and said we gots till Saturday to get out or be burned out, or worse."

"The Klan?" said Chock. "I thought that kind of thing had died out years ago."

"I guess not when it comes to me rather than a white boy workin' for you. Least that's what the Klan boys said."

"Well that's not right. You're working for me because you know your job and you work hard and you're dependable. Besides, I make the decision on who works for me and who doesn't. Most of those town loafers wouldn't know a spud wrench from a jack stand and would probably injure themselves before learning the difference between the two. You say the Klan boys said they would give you till Saturday to clear out?"

"Yes sir, said they'd be back Saturday night to burn us out or string me up."

"Well, we'll have to see about that. You go on to work. I'll talk to Bull and we'll work this thing out," said Chock.

"Did Collin say if he recognized any of the cowards?" asked Bull. Chock had relayed Collin's experience the previous night to Bull in his office.

"No, it was dark and they were all in hoods and robes. Besides, he was so scared his wife and family were going to be hurt, I don't think he was able to concentrate on anything like that."

"Probably brought in from Buford County. I heard the Klan had started up a group over there. Guess they're trying to show some muscle to help recruit over here. Bud and I may just need to pay a visit to Collin's place on Saturday night," said Bull.

Bull's lone Deputy, Bud Leighton, was known throughout the county as a fearless law enforcement agent. Rumor had it that he had once been charged with killing a man up north but that Bull had pulled strings to get the charges dismissed. There were even rumors that Bud was somehow related to Bull, but no one knew for certain and no one asked. It was well-known that Bud was honest and totally loyal to Bull. Anyone who crossed Bull knew they would not only have that staunch lawman to deal with but also would have to face Bud Leighton. That certainty kept many a criminal reluctant to conduct business in Bull's county.

"Fine, I'll go with you," said Chock.

"No need for that, Bud and I can handle it."

"I'm sure you can but this is a case where I've been branded as the cause as well as Collin. They need to know I won't stand for Collin to be threatened or scared into hiring one of their kind and the best way for them to know it is to see me there too."

"Okay, suit yourself, but Bud and I will do the talking, you just lend your support by being there. Meet us here right after supper on Saturday. We'll get there before dark and get set up."

On the way out to Collin's place on Saturday evening, the three men were silent. The roads were rough as the county didn't spend a lot of money keeping them in good condition in the back roads area. As they arrived, Collin met them in the front yard. "I sent Carrie and the kids over to stay with her sister and husband in Delford," said Collin. "They're pretty scared and it's better for them not to be here."

"Good," said Bull. "Let's get in the house and see how this is going to play out."

Flames jumped from the large bonfire causing the tall white cross to look as though it was moving in the early evening. A large group of men were pulling on their hoods and robes as the moon rose above the tree line, adding even more eerie lights to the scene.

Gordon Brown was taking a long drag from the first jarful of moonshine as the men around him were donning their hoods and robes. Other jars were being passed around and after each pull, the obligatory, "Damn that's good stuff, where'd you get it Skeeter?" was followed by, "You know better than to ask, just be glad it's free," from Skeeter, at which they all laughed as one. It was a known fact that when a clavern was seeking recruits, the moonshine flowed free and easy. As Skeeter handed the jar around, he stated, "Now, let's just figure that nigger done cleared out and all we're gonna do is have a little shack torchin.'"

"Yeah, but what if he ain't gone?" asked Gordon.

Another of the hooded Klansmen cracked a long, black whip and said, "Well, we'll just have to give him a little more persuasion."

Another held up a pre-tied noose and said, "By the time we pull him around by this a few times and Danny gets his whip on his black ass, he'll damn well wish he had left a month ago."

They all laughed but Gordon asked again, "What if he's got a gun or something?"

At which one of the Klansmen pulled up his robe to show a handgun stuck into his belt. "We'll deal with that too if necessary!"

"Okay, everybody, let's get goin' – the moon's already up and we don't need to be out too late. Remember, there's church tomorrow." At which they all laughed loudly.

Collin sat motionless on the porch swing. At half past nine, he saw the car lights turn off the main road. He could see lighted torches on both sides of the three cars as they came down the lane. His house lay in complete darkness. The din of frogs croaking and June bugs buzzing were the only sounds until the car tires crunched on the gravel in front of the house. The hooded and robed men emerged from the cars and came to stand twenty feet in front of the house. The flames from the torches danced and cast eerie shadows onto the porch. "Thought we told you to get out the other night," growled one of the hoods.

Collin slowly stood up and faced the crowd of men. "Guess you did, but I didn't believe it was your right to order us to leave so I decided to stay."

"So did we," said Bull as he stepped through the dark door of the shack followed closely by Bud and Chock. Bull and Bud each cradled a sawed-off shotgun in the crooks of their arms. The torch light reflected back from their badges and for a moment, no one said anything.

"Now listen here, Bull, this ain't none of your affair, this is between us and that nigger. He's been out of line and we're settin' him straight."

"Well, now, that's where you're wrong," said Bull. "I've known Collin for over ten years. Never had no reason to ever cross hairs with him. All he does is work, take care of his family and go to church. Now in my book that doesn't warrant being run out of town."

"He's still a nigger and he's takin' a white man's job."

"He's only doing the job he's trained to do and doing it well," said Chock. "Some of you could learn a lesson in how to conduct your lives by taking a good look at Collin Jones."

At this one of the torches from the back came cartwheeling through the air toward the porch. Bull fired his shotgun into the air, knocking it down and yelled, "Back off!" at which two more torches were hurled at the porch.

Chock kicked at a torch and in so doing knocked it back at the Klansmen. A pistol shot rang out and Chock pitched forward.

Mass confusion broke out. More torches were being hurled at the porch – Bud raised his shotgun and let go with Bull yelling, "NO, NO."

More pistol shots rang out. Collin dived for the ground, Bud went down to one knee with another shotgun blast digging up the dirt ten feet in front of him. The cars were tearing out of the driveway with Klansmen partially in and partially out. Bull was on his knees at Chock's side moaning, "No, no, don't let this happen." Chock's eyes glazed over as he saw Collin kneeling over him and Bull with tears flowing freely down his cheeks. One last gasp and a short sigh and Chock Dillard was dead.

CHAPTER TWENTY-TWO

Hendley, Texas   *Summer 1922*

The heat shimmered off the roadway as the hearse made its way into the cemetery. Somehow, it just didn't seem right that the sun shone, people talked, birds flew, grass grew and Poppa was gone. It was like time ticked by but nothing really mattered. Kathy May wished she were dead. Poppa was gone. Sara May just stared straight ahead not saying a word. Kathy May's Aunt June had come to stay with them for the grieving time. Sara May didn't seem to notice although Aunt June prattled on about everything and nothing. The car they were riding in came to a stop behind the hearse and everyone climbed out and began to assemble around the open grave. There were two rows of chairs under the shade of a tree and all assembled there to hear Pastor Edwards deliver Kathy May's poppa's eulogy.

The pastor began, "It is at a time like this when you may think we have the right to ask why? And when you ask, there is no satisfactory answer. Because there is no way to know the plan of the Lord. He calls us to his side for his own reason, not for ours. Our time on earth is but a fleeting moment in God's grand scheme of things. We do know that Chock Dillard died doing a noble thing. He was standing up for a friend, a man he knew and believed could use his support. Chock knew there was a danger in his actions. But the importance of showing his support for another human being outweighed that danger. Now don't get me wrong. I don't believe Chock Dillard went to stand up for Collin Jones thinking that he would have to give up his life. He went because he believed it was the right thing to do. That was the way Chock lived his life. He believed in doing the right thing. Chock is in a better place – a place where there is no discrimination – no hate – no fear of being spit upon but a place of love and forgiveness. The Lord teaches us to love one another, turn the other cheek, be kind to your neighbor, and keep faith in the Father, the Son and the Holy Spirit. It is at times like this when our faith is most sorely tested. Chock Dillard did not deserve to die. Our solace is knowing that the Lord has a better place for Chock – and he is there with him now. Let us pray."

Pastor Edwards prayed a long time. He had worked up a pretty good sweat by the time he finished and he mopped at his brow with his pocket handkerchief. He bent down to Sara May and said how sorry he was but she just stared and did not respond. Bull and the other people slowly began to move away from the shade toward their cars. All the while, Sara May just continued to sit and stare.

Finally, Aunt June said, "Sara, it's time to go – it's time to leave."

Sara May still didn't acknowledge hearing anything but slowly stood and continued to stare. As she looked at Chock's casket suspended above the grave, it was as though she was seeing it for the first time. "Why are we here?" she asked. "Has someone died?"

Bull was at her side and said, "It's okay, Sara May, but I do believe you've been out in the hot sun a little too long. Come on to the car and have a drink of water."

Sara May allowed him to guide her back to the car and help her inside. The blank stare had returned and she sat motionless in the back seat.

Kathy May heard Bull telling Aunt June that she should get Dr. Hurling to take a look at Sara May. Aunt June replied, "Yes, we'll do that tomorrow. Let's just get her home for now and let her lie down."

The ride home was long with Sara May staring and Aunt June prattling on about the service – how Pastor Edwards had said all the right things. Sara May asked again, "Has someone died?" and Aunt June just sat with her mouth open. Finally, Kathy May said, "Mama, Poppa died – he went away." She stared at Kathy May with no comprehension of what she had just said.

When they got home, Aunt June tried to get Sara May to lie down to rest, but she just kept saying, "No, I've got to get a pitcher of iced tea made for Chock. You know how he likes it strong and sweet. He'll be coming home any time now and he likes his iced tea on a hot day." She heated a pan of water and got out the tea pitcher to mix it in. All the time, Aunt June just sat and kept shaking her head. Bull finally took Sara May by the shoulders and looked straight into her eyes and said, "Sara May, I know you loved Chock with all your heart, but he's gone and you need to accept it – you need to snap out of this dream you're having."

Sara May simply stared and kept saying she needed to get the iced tea ready for Chock – "He'll be coming home any time now." Finally, Bull released her shoulders and just shook his head. She returned to the ritual of making the pitcher of iced tea just as she had done hundreds of times. Bull said to Aunt June, "Maybe she'll snap out of it in a day or two. In the meantime, I think you need to stay here with her and Kathy May. I'll make arrangements for Dr. Hurling to come out tomorrow to take a look."

"Yes, that will be best. In the meantime, we'll just humor her and not cause any more stress in her situation."

Bull nodded, picked up his hat, gave Aunt June a peck on the cheek as he left through the front door.

Sara May had finished making the pitcher of tea and carried it and two goblets to a small table on the front porch. She pulled up a wood chair next to the table and sat down with an air of expectation. "He'll be along any time now," she kept saying almost to herself.

When dark came, Aunt June helped her up to her bedroom and helped her undress for bed. Sara May just kept saying, "No, I'll wait for Chock, he'll be along soon."

Aunt June did not argue but just kept rattling on about everything but Chock. Kathy May just sat and watched. She couldn't get through to her mother either.

Sara May was so devastated by Chock's death, she couldn't accept his death and just felt all tight and broken inside. Kathy May kept hugging her and saying it would be all right although she knew it would never be all right with her again. Finally, from utter exhaustion, Sara May fell asleep. Kathy May crawled into bed with her and held her and cried herself to sleep.

The next day, when Dr. Hurling arrived, Sara May was at her table on the porch with a pitcher of iced tea and two drinking goblets saying, "He'll be along any time now." Dr. Hurling examined Sara May with care and feeling. It didn't seem to make any difference what he asked, she only answered about waiting for Chock to come home. Bull drove up and came onto the porch. He and Aunt June just looked at each other and Aunt June slowly shook her head. When Dr. Hurling had finished, he and Bull stepped down off the porch and he spoke in a hushed voice to Bull for a few minutes. He then asked Kathy May to come and talk to him.

The two of them walked to his car, he opened the door and set his examination case into the back seat. Finally he turned and said, "Kathy May, your Mama's mind just cannot accept the loss of Chock and she is closing everything else off."

Kathy May told him that her mama had not even acknowledged her existence since she was told of Chock's death.

"There is so much we don't know about the human mind, she may just come back to us quickly or maybe never. I believe we should have her admitted to the sanitarium at San Antonio. They have doctors and nurses trained to work with cases like this and they may be able to help her. I don't know how to treat this kind of illness. I spoke with Bull and he and Mary would like for you to stay with them while your mama is away. Would that be all right with you?"

Kathy May nodded and said, "I would like that."

Dr. Hurling said he would make the arrangements to have Sara May admitted to the sanitarium the next day and she should pack clothes for her stay with Bull and Mary.

Sara May never did recover from Chock's death. She just slowly wasted away at the sanitarium. They said her grief was so great and the wall of denial so strong, they just could never reach her. She died a year and a day after she had been admitted.

CHAPTER TWENTY-THREE

Hendley, Texas   *Winter 1922*

B ud Leighton was dog tired. He had been on duty for a solid
week tracking down leads on moonshiners in the back country
of the county. It was debatable whether, when he and his group
found a hidden still and destroyed it, it was a success or a failure.
Most stills were developed to bring a little extra income for some
struggling, downtrodden farmer whose farm teetered on the edge
of failure. In destroying the stills, they may also be sending its owner
into failure and bankruptcy and certainly making a bitter enemy
against the lawmen saddled with the job of destruction. On rare
occasions, Bud and his fellow deputies would encounter the still's
owners and arrest them as well as destroy their illicit operations.
Most of the time, there was no one around and the landowner
would deny any knowledge of the existence or ownership of the
still. Most of them did not want to know anything about the illegal

operations, even when on occasion a couple of jugs of "shine" were left on their back porches in the middle of the night.

Bud entered the café near closing time and located an unoccupied table near the rear in a corner which was where he preferred to sit. It was not well-lit and he could monitor many of the conversations taking place in the restaurant, becoming almost invisible in the remote corner. He ordered a serving of the house specialty, corned beef hash and eggs, with a cup of the strong, black coffee always available at the café. A group of four young men entered and took a table near the center of the café. Bud was slowly consuming his food, and looked up to recognize two in the group, Skeeter Brown and Joey Bailey. They did not seem to notice Bud's presence. A few of the other diners finished their meals, paid their checks and exited the café, leaving only three or four tables occupied in addition to the table of four and Bud at his lone table. Bud's ears perked up when he heard one of the young guys mention the possibility of another Klan roust out. They mentioned a black man's name who resided in a neighboring county, which Bud had heard of. He became really interested when Skeeter Brown said something about a chance to clear up rumors on the Chock Dillard shooting.

One of the men who Bud did not know asked Skeeter, "Think you could get us four or five jugs of shine to help bolster the new boys' courage?" Skeeter replied that it should be possible as long as they didn't screw up the rousting out of this nigger. They turned their attention to consuming their food and the conversation turned to other topics generally not of interest to Bud.

After they left, Bud withdrew a notepad from his coat pocket and recorded the details of the discussion he had overheard, noted the date, location and time as well as the names Skeeter Brown and Joey Bailey plus two unknowns. Bud paid his bill and left the café.

He walked the two blocks to the Sheriff's office, entered and found Bull at his desk. "You won't believe what I just overheard down at the Wheel-in," said Bud as he extracted his pad from his coat pocket. "Skeeter Brown and Joey Bailey appear to have been present at the Collin Jones fracas when Chock was killed. This is the first time we've heard someone refer to the night they threatened Collin and killed Chock," said Bud.

Bull replied, "Well, it's a lead but we still don't know who actually shot Chock, but it may be enough to put them in jail and try to sweat more names out of them. I'll speak to the judge tomorrow morning and see if we can get a warrant issued for their arrest. For now, about all we would have on them would be trespassing and engaging in an illegal assembly, but at least it's a start."

The following morning Bull announced, "I've got the warrants for you. Get a couple of the other deputies and go bring those two in," said Bull to Bud. "Don't shoot them if you don't have to. We need them to talk, not die," said Bull.

"This will be a real pleasure," said Bud. "This Skeeter kid has been a total pain in the ass of this town for as long as I've been here."

It was rumored that Bud had been hired to help end the Colorado range wars in the early part of the century. A dozen men had been killed and rumor had it that Bud had been involved, but no one knew for sure which side he was on. He had simply drifted into town not too long after Bull was first elected Sheriff, and saw a sign on the Sheriff's door advertising for deputies to be hired. He entered, applied and was hired pretty much only on the story he told Bull, which Bull had relayed only to the County Commissioner to secure his approval to put Bud on the payroll.

The next day, Bull and Bud sat on one side of the table with Skeeter Brown and his lawyer on the other side. "Now let me get this straight," said Bull, "You say that you and a group of your friends only went to Collin Jones' place to try and collect some back rent Collin owed to your father who owned the house occupied by Collin and his family, and you figured you could scare him into paying up by pretending to be the KKK? Now that's about the biggest load of crap I've ever heard. Did you forget that both Bud and I were present at that meeting and we heard what was said?" advised Bull.

"Well that's what it was about but everything went out of control when the two of you stepped out with those sawed-off shotguns pointing at us," said Skeeter.

"There was never any mention of back rent and we can check courthouse records as to the ownership of the house and land," said Bull.

"Go ahead and check, you'll see that what I said is true. There never was any plan to actually force Collin to leave, just catch up on the rent," said Skeeter. "There's no need to go any further," said the lawyer to Skeeter. "Leave it at that." Turning to Bull he added, "Since Skeeter's father owns the land, there's no basis for your trespassing charge or for an illegal assembly."

"They still need to testify about Chock's death. Someone in that group shot Chock and we intend to find out who it was," said Bull.

"They've already told you they don't know who shot Chock. Anyway, we would contend it was in self-defense as you fired your shotgun at the crowd first," said the lawyer.

"Not true," stated Bull. "I shot a torch out of the air that had been thrown at the porch."

"These boys will swear that you fired in the direction of the crowd and caused general chaos," said the lawyer. "We'll shoot so many holes in your case that it won't hold up in court. It'll be thrown out and you may be subject to a charge of causing the whole thing," he added.

"We'll let these two out but don't leave town while we're checking out their story," said Bull to Bud.

After they had all left, Bud said, "You know they're lying and we can't do anything about it as long as they're willing to lie under oath. We'll just have to keep trying to find some other way to handle this."

Six months later, Bud Leighton and his deputies raided another still and Skeeter Brown was killed when he tried to run from the raid. The deputies all agreed they had tried to lawfully apprehend Skeeter but he had resisted arrest and they feared for their lives. A court of inquiry did not find any fault with the deputies' handling of the matter.

Secretly, Bud and Bull felt Chock's death had been at least partially solved. They still didn't know who actually fired the shot that killed Chock, but at least the organizer of the group had been brought down. Sometimes you just have to accept a partial resolution to an unfortunate occurrence.

Kathy May came to love Bull and Mary. Mary welcomed Kathy May almost as though she was her own child and in fact always treated her in that manner. She and Bull served as surrogate parents all through her years of growing up and attending college. They acted as conservators for the steady stream of income being received in the form of drilling royalties from the numerous oil wells her father had developed, primarily with Native American landowners.

Upon graduation from college, she returned to Hendley and accepted a teacher's job at the same school where Mary was teaching. They were inseparable and took many trips together to experience the pleasures of play performances, operas and museum tours.

At the age of forty-one, Mary began to experience more tiredness and a lack of energy. She never complained but it became obvious that something was wrong. Bull took her to a variety of clinics and doctors, but there was no definitive diagnosis from any they visited. Eventually, she just sort of gave up and remained bedridden for most of her remaining days.

One morning, she simply did not come out of her room and when Bull went to investigate, he found her lifeless and gone from this world. For months, Bull was barely able to function, suffering the degree of grief which had descended upon him the day his Mary left him. He began to drink heavily and his friends could not bring him out of his depression. Kathy May was the only one he would converse with and then generally only about the things she and his Mary had done together.

Five months later, as he sat in the Sheriff's office and thought about his state of life, a stranger entered. Bull was slightly drunk and asked the stranger if he needed any help.

At this, the stranger pulled a pistol from his pocket and asked, "Are you Ruell Pierce, the gunman who killed those two bank robbers years ago?"

Ruell slowly nodded his head yes, looked up at the stranger and asked, "Who are you?"

"Those three guys were my cousins. I've thought about that all these years and have to figure you somehow got an unfair drop on them. There's no way you could have killed two and knocked out the third one without some kind of trick," said the stranger.

"No trick, just straight quick shooting," said Bull at which the stranger fired three bullets into Bull's heart. Bull never even tried to pull his gun.

Life is full of many strange twists and turns. Certainly, Ruell Pierce's life took many twists and turns, even changing his name from Ruell to Bull. Some could even contend Bull's fate was set by a mule's fart when he was fifteen years old. Who can say?

CHAPTER TWENTY-FOUR

Hendley, Texas   *Summer 1923*

Bud Leighton opened the door marked Chief County Commissioner in the County Courthouse. The receptionist smiled as he introduced himself and she stated how shocked everyone was over Bull's death. "Thank you," said Bud. "He was a really good man and an honest lawman. We all really miss him. I'm here to see Chief Commissioner Bryan Jenkins."

"Yes, he's expecting you. Please go on in," advised the receptionist.

Bud entered the inner office and saw the Chief Commissioner rising from behind his desk, holding a thick law book in his hands. Bud was surprised at the Commissioner's appearance. He was a small man, no more than five feet, four inches tall with a slender build. His hair was gray and thinning and he wore a pair of glasses which seemed to pinch his nose. "Thanks for coming, Bud. We all extend our sincerest sympathy for Bull's death. He was well-liked and respected throughout the entire county."

"We all miss him every day," said Bud. "What can I do to help you?"

"The Board of Commissioners met last night and voted to schedule a special election to replace Bull to be held no sooner than ninety days from today. In the meantime, the Board has asked that you take the job of interim Sheriff until the election is held," said the Commissioner.

"Well, sure," said Bud. "What's the process?"

"Just hold up your right hand and repeat after me," said the Commissioner. "I (state your name) do solemnly swear that I will faithfully execute the duties of the office of interim Sheriff of the State of Texas, and will to the best of my ability preserve, protect and defend the Constitution and laws of the United States and of this State, so help me God."

After being sworn in, Bud said, "Just so you know, my highest priority is in finding the person or person's responsible for Bull's death."

"We expected that would be your first priority and we wish you Godspeed in that endeavor. Take a look at your other deputies and assign as much of the day-to-day duties as possible to them," said the Commissioner.

"Already thought that out," said Bud. "It'll be in operation tomorrow."

"Do you have any leads on the murderer yet?" asked the Commissioner.

"Nothing solid yet," said Bud, "but a couple of possibilities do exist. The thing that comes to mind first could be related to or associated with one or both of the bank robbers Bull killed before becoming Sheriff."

"I do recall hearing about that at the time," said the Commissioner. "Seems like I heard there was a third fellow involved in that robbery. What's become of him?"

"Bull once told me the third robber was the one who dropped his gun onto the floor which Bull was able to grab and shoot the first two and then he tackled and knocked out the third guy," said Bud. "He was tried and sentenced to thirty years in prison and is serving his time in the state prison at Butcher Creek. I'm planning to take a drive over the day after tomorrow and see what, if anything, I can get from him."

"Well, we wish you the best of luck and please keep us informed of your progress," said the Commissioner.

"I will," said Bud. "I need for you to keep any information developed in this matter totally confidential. Can't have anyone know who we are checking on," said Bud.

Bud spent the next day at the courthouse checking all details and records on the trial he had discussed with the Commissioner. He learned the criminal's name was Clyde Harris. His two dead accomplices were Harry and John Barton, brothers. The Barton brothers had grown up in the Wichita Falls, Texas, area. Harris was a drifter from the ranch area near Wichita Falls. They had robbed five banks together before running into Bull Pierce, who ended their lawless careers. Bud had called and spoken with the Warden at the Butcher Creek Prison and received permission to visit with Clyde Harris. The Warden advised they had been holding Harris for fourteen years and he had not caused any problems.

Bud was escorted to the Warden's office at the prison and he was impressed with Warden Brown's firm handshake and no-nonsense attitude. He told Bud, "I run a clean, orderly prison. Most of the men sent here accept their sentences and serve their time, staying out of trouble. Occasionally, we get a real hard-ass and sometimes they don't last too long. If they cause problems, the other prisoners isolate them out and sometimes bad things happen to them. The word gets out – cause problems and get your neck slit – most of them knuckle down, do their time and try to go straight when they get released. Some of them don't make it and end up back here. Sometimes, more than once. You see I believe most men don't plan to break the law. Some just don't have the skills to make it on the outside and turn to lawlessness just to survive. That's the case with Clyde Harris. No real education, no family support, on his own at an early age, stealing to get by. He thought he and the Barton brothers were going to get big money from robbing banks. I understand he had $10 on his person when he was cold-cocked by your friend Bull Pierce."

"That's pretty much it," said Bud. "I want to talk to Harris to see if he has any idea on who would want to bring harm to Bull for ending their bank-robbing careers."

"Good luck to you. I looked up the visitor logs on him and in the last ten years, he has had one visitor on two occasions."

"And who might that be?" asked Bud.

"Name was Joe Barton from Wichita Falls."

"Very interesting," said Bud.

The guard escorted Bud to a visitor's area which had six small tables set up with chairs on each side. A lady was crying while speaking to a man who sat glumly across the table from her with his hands manacled together. An unarmed prison guard stood inside the door while the guard who escorted Bud to the center remained outside. "Go in, take a seat and he'll be brought out to you shortly." This guard was armed with a .45 pistol. He explained to Bud that armed guards were not allowed to enter the visitor area unless there was a problem. There were few problems.

Bud eased himself into a wood chair at the table farthest away from the crying lady. Crying ladies made Bud nervous. His mother and sisters had cried when he left home to go on his own at sixteen, and it had been an unhappy experience.

Soon, the door at the rear of the room opened and an unarmed guard escorted Clyde Harris to the table. Bud did not stand or offer to shake hands with Harris. As he sat down, Bud asked, "How you making out in here?"

"I get by," said Harris. "Now who the hell are you?"

Bud gave Harris a quick rundown and when he mentioned Bull Pierce, Harris jerked back. "Pierce!" said Harris. "That's the guy who put me in here and killed my two buddies, but his name was Ruell."

Bud told the story of how Ruell had been renamed Bull, at which Harris laughed and said, "Maybe he wasn't such a bad bastard after all."

"He wasn't," said Bud, "but somebody hated him enough to put three bullets in his heart as he sat at his desk."

Harris did not react with any surprise and Bud was pretty sure Harris knew at least one person capable of killing Bull. "You wouldn't happen to know anyone who would be pleased to know Bull was killed?" asked Bud.

"I don't think any of the Barton clan would be sorry to hear about that," said Harris.

"Yeah, but any of them actually capable of doing the job?" asked Bud.

"Even if I knew, what makes you think I'd tell you?" asked Harris.

"The Warden tells me you keep your nose clean and stay out of trouble. Any help you provide and I'll put in a good word with the Warden and you might get to be made a trustee. You know, help with delivering meals, in the laundry and so forth. Also, you'd get first crack at food at mealtime with no short rations," said Bud.

At that Harris said, "You ever shoot pool?"

Bud leaned back in his chair and said, "I've been known to shoot a little pool. Never played billiards though."

"You oughta take another shot at shooting pool," said Harris as he rose from the chair, nodded to the guard at the door at the end of the room and shuffled to the rear of the room. He never looked back.

Now what the hell does that mean, wondered Bud, as he rose and motioned to the guard at the entry door.

As he was leaving, he was again escorted to the Warden's office. Warden Brown asked, "Was he of any help?"

After Bud had sat down and reached for the cup of coffee offered by the Warden, he replied, "Not sure, he didn't act all that surprised when I told him that Bull had been killed. All he said was that I should shoot some pool."

At this the Warden laughed, slapped his thigh and said, "Well, I'll be damned."

Bud said, "Does that mean anything to you?"

The Warden smiled and said, "You know how we search all visitors arriving and leaving?"

"Yes, standard prison policy," said Bud.

"Well, each time Joe Barton visited, he had a cube of pool stick chalk in his pocket."

Bud smiled and said, "You know, you just might take a look at making Mr. Harris a trustee."

The Warden said, "Let me know how you do at shooting pool."

Bud Leighton drove the forty-five miles to Wichita Falls the next day. He drove easy and carefully. He left his policing authority at the county line and he felt almost naked. This was the first time he had left the comfort of being a law enforcement agent in twelve years, and it felt strange. He did not leave his .45 side arm back in Hendley. It was firmly seated in the shoulder holster which he wore on occasion to conceal his weapon. Bud felt certain he would be able to locate Joe Barton, but just what would he do with him when he found him? It was quite unlikely he would be able to get him to confess to knowing anything about Bull Pierce's death. And furthermore, what would he do if he did admit to knowing anything? Even with all his doubts, Bud was drawn to find Joe Barton much as a moth is drawn to a light.

As Bud reached the city limits of Wichita Falls, he was impressed with the size of the city. In his previous wanderings, he had once passed through the city and it now appeared to have almost doubled in size. There were numerous new homes being constructed and Bud drove toward the city center with a growing feeling of confidence. He had no trouble locating the sleazy part of the downtown. The street had numerous joints, domino parlors and a half-dozen pool halls. One of the pool halls had the name "Barton's Pool and Dominoes" above the door.

"Gotta be the place," said Bud to himself. A vague outline of a plan to get Joe Barton to come to him had started forming in Bud's mind.

He found parking for his car a block from the pool hall. Bud entered a pool hall a block south of Barton's place. The name above the door was Harry's Place. The hall had six pool tables and two were occupied by various men shooting pool with some dollar bills placed on the end railing of the tables. As one contestant won his game, he picked up the bills and turned to the half dozen onlookers and asked, "Anyone else ready to take on the Eight Ball King?"

"Not for money," said one.

"Well, that's the only way I play this game. How about you?" said the Eight Ball King as he pointed his pool cue at Bud.

"No, no, I'm just passing through," said Bud. "Just looking to buy some cattle and waiting for the boss to make it into town."

"I'll make it easy for you, a dollar a ball plus five for a win," said the Eight Ball King.

"My mama always told me, 'Never play poker with a guy named Slim or shoot pool with a guy named Eight Ball King,'" said Bud.

The Eight Ball King laughed and said, "How about if my name was really Paul Anderson and not the Eight Ball King?"

"Now, that's a different thing. She never said to not play against a guy named Paul," said Bud.

The pool hustler laughed and said, "You know, I think I would have liked your mama. She would probably want to mother all us lost wayward orphans."

Bud nodded as he extracted a dozen dollar bills from his wallet and set them on the end rail of the pool table. "Winner pays the hall a dollar a game," said the hustler.

"Fine by me," said Bud. "Let's flip for the break, heads I break, tails you break."

Bud won the toss and lined up his opening shot with care and sent balls running in all directions on the pool table. The three ball fell into a mid-pocket. The game of eight ball now would require Bud to continue shooting at only the remaining six balls numbered less than eight. His opponent would be required to shoot only the balls numbered nine to fifteen. To continue to shoot, each player would be allowed to shoot as long as he continued to knock his balls into a table pocket. If the player missed sinking a ball or if his cue ball shot struck one of his opponent's balls first, he would lose his turn and the opponent would be allowed to continue attempting to put his balls into the six pockets on the table. After shooting all his designated balls into the pockets, the player would be required to "call" his final shot on the eight ball. This meant the player had to call the pocket he was planning to shoot the eight ball into and also announce if it was to be a banked shot or if the eight ball was to ricochet off one of his opponent's balls. If the player failed to make his called shot on the eight ball, he would simply lose his turn and his opponent would try to "run" the table. Should the eight ball fall into any pocket other than the called pocket, the player automatically would lose the game. If the player is successful with his called eight-ball shot, he would win the game. There are numerous variations to the game of eight ball, but these are the most commonly followed.

Bud then dropped his six, seven and one balls into various pockets. His shot at the two ball missed slightly and he said to Paul, "Your table, run it if you can."

Paul grinned as he leaned over the table and lined up his first shot. "Not bad shooting for an opening round," he said. "Now, let me show you how it's done." Paul methodically pocketed all his balls except for the twelve and fifteen. The twelve ball was hidden behind the eight ball and the fifteen was not a clean shot. Paul carefully banked his cue ball off the side rail and it nicked the front side of the fifteen ball, which came to rest two inches from an end pocket. He grimaced and stepped back from the table. Bud calmly leaned over the table and dropped the two and four balls into an end pocket.

The cue ball rolled to a gentle stop some three feet from the eight ball. "Eight ball, corner pocket off your fifteen," said Bud, as he moved to the middle of the table. A light yet firm stroke of the cue stick sent the cue ball knocking the eight ball toward the end pocket and just lightly ticked the fifteen ball before dropping softly into the called pocket.

"Nice game," said Paul. "I do believe you have played this game before."

"On a few occasions but generally not for money," lied Bud as he picked up the bills from the end of the table. He walked over to the counterman and said, "You've got a nice table there, straight and true," as he dropped $2 onto the counter.

"Best quality in town," announced the counterman.

"Besides the Eight Ball King, who else in town shoots a good game of pool?" asked Bud.

"Well, Joe Barton down the street won last year's tournament so I'd have to say he's pretty good," said the counterman.

"If he gets the break, his opponent generally never gets to shoot."

"That sounds like a talented pool player," said Bud.

"If you think you're going to play him, you'd better take a few more turns with the Eight Ball King. He came in second."

Bud turned back to the Eight Ball King, "How about it, you up for a couple more games?"

"If you'll let me win a few, I'll play," answered the Eight Ball King.

"I could say the same to you," responded Bud.

They played eight more games with Bud winning five and the Eight Ball King three. At which Bud announced he was turning in for the night, and he prepared to leave. As he was going out the door, the Eight Ball King yelled out, "Come back anytime."

Bud drove a few blocks away from the downtown area, spotted a boarding house, parked his car and went into the boarding house. An elderly man was behind a desk and greeted him with a smile.

"Got any rooms available?" asked Bud.

"Sure, how long you intending to stay?" answered the clerk.

"No more than a week. Just waiting to meet up with my boss who will be coming in to purchase some cattle."

"Room Fourteen is available for $15 a week. Just pay in advance and sign the register," said the clerk as he pushed a register book across the desk. Bud did as requested, signed the register as Bud Walker, paid the $15 in advance and received a room key with a round label numbered Fourteen, and marched up the stairs.

"Any good places to eat around here?" called Bud over his shoulder at the top of the stairs.

"Sure, Margie's is just down the street a couple of blocks. Serves good home-cooked food," responded the clerk.

"Thanks," answered Bud as he made his way down the hallway to Room Fourteen.

The next morning Bud went to the stockyard area and visited with the manager. He further enhanced his story about being a front man for his boss who would be coming to Wichita Falls in a few days to purchase a substantial number of cattle. He was careful to never disclose anything that could be checked on by any of the people he spoke with. His plan to get to Joe Barton was forming up nicely.

In the afternoon, he returned to Harry's Place and shot more games of pool with the Eight Ball King. Occasionally a mild question pertaining to Joe Barton provided more information. He learned that Joe was part of a large local family regarded as tough. The townspeople knew that two of his cousins had been killed while attempting to rob a bank at Hendley. There were various stories about the details of the killing and robbery attempt. Some sympathetic to the Bartons, some not. He casually dropped information about his discussions with the stockyard manager and more hints of his boss coming to town to purchase cattle. Two thousand head at $65 each would require a substantial sum of money.

"No problem," said Bud. "The boss has plenty of money. Never carries much on his person as he is afraid it could attract bad people."

"How does he get funds transferred to handle that large of a purchase?" asked one member of the pool hall crowd.

"Special anonymous courier," advised Bud. "He'll bring it into town and set up an account at one of the local banks a few days before the boss is scheduled to arrive."

Bud also learned that Barton was married but had no children. It was rumored that he and his wife fought frequently, generally about her desire to spend more money than Barton thought appropriate.

Bud played pool with a few other patrons but none were as talented as the Eight Ball King. Over a period of a few days, Bud and the Eight Ball King grew to like and respect each other. Bud would laugh helplessly when, upon entering an establishment, the Eight Ball King would yell out, "I'm the Eight Ball King and I'm hell when I'm well and I ain't NEVER been sick!" At the next joint he would announce, "I'm the Eight Ball King and I'm a mean sumbitch when I'm drinkin' and I'm ALWAYS drinkin' just a little bit." No one ever challenged the King's pronouncements. They just laughed with him and went back to doing what they were doing before he arrived. On Saturday, the two of them went into Barton's pool hall and shot a couple of games of pool, each one winning once. Eventually, Joe Barton sidled up to the King and asked, "This that hot shot I been hearing about beating you at pool?"

The King leaned back from his turn at the pool table and said, "Joe, this here is Bud Walker, in town for a few days and, yes, we have shot a few games. He wins sometimes and I win sometimes."

"Think he can beat me?" asked Barton.

"You should play him and find out for yourself," answered the King.

At this Bud said, "Heck no, I don't think I can beat you but I'm willing to try if you are."

Barton said, "I don't play for fun."

"Well that's fine by me. What kind of wager you have in mind?

"How about $1,000 each," said Barton.

"Now that's a serious wager. I don't have that kind of money with me," responded Bud. "I'd be willing to take your IOU. I hear your boss is due in town soon and if I win, you can pay me then," said Barton. "I just want to take you down a notch or two. I'm top dog in this town when it comes to pool."

Bud said, "Okay, just straight eight-ball pool for $1,000."

"That's right, and I never lose," said Barton.

Word quickly spread as the size of the wager was substantial, and soon the hall was filling with onlookers. The Eight Ball King had stationed himself at the entrance and, always the hustler, was charging entrants $5 each to gain entry into the hall. Bud and Barton faced each other like a couple of prizefighters ready to enter the ring and spar for a championship. Barton flipped a half dollar onto the pool table and called "heads" as it spun in the air. It hit the table, bounced and came to rest showing tails. Bud applied chalk to the tip of his pool cue, leaned over the end of the table, set the cue ball near the limit line and said, "Here goes," as he drew his cue back and sent the cue ball rocketing into the first ball on the racked set. Balls flew around the table and the fifteen ball rolled into a far end pocket. Bud coolly ran the remaining balls on the table into the six table pockets. At each shot, a hush settled over the crowd and a cheer arose each time a ball fell into a pocket. Finally, all nine through fifteen balls had been pocketed. Only Barton's one through seven balls and the eight ball remained on the table. Bud called out, "Eight ball, side pocket, one bank." Bud inhaled a deep breath, expelled it and leaned onto the table. Someone yelled, "Both feet on the floor or you scratch." Bud pulled back, looked at Barton and asked, "Is that right? I didn't hear anything about that."

"Hall rules," replied Barton as he pointed to a paper mounted above the counter titled "Hall Rules."

Bud moved to the counter and could just barely read the typed paper. Sure enough, rule eight stated, "A player shall maintain both feet on the floor while in the act of shooting. Violation of this rule shall result in the player being automatically disqualified from the match and an automatic win for his opponent."

Bud reviewed the other posted rules, and seeing no other surprises, he returned to the pool table. Looking in the direction of the man who had alerted him to the rule, he said, "Thanks," and returned to his place at the side of the table. As he leaned over the table, he looked over his shoulder at Barton, then down to the floor where both feet were firmly planted and finally back to lining up his shot on the eight ball.

Again, Bud called out, "Eight ball, side pocket, one bank." He drew the cue stick back and sent the cue ball at the eight with a short sure stroke. Crack went the ball as it struck the eight ball which bounced off the rail and rolled across the table and dropped into the side pocket with a thud. The crowd went wild as various wagers were paid off between observers. The Eight Ball King was busy collecting his winnings from three of Barton's cronies. Barton stuck his cue stick into the rack attached to the wall.

"How about another game? Give me a chance to break even," said Barton to Bud.

"Not today. I'm afraid I'm only good for one $1,000 match per day," responded Bud.

At this, Barton motioned for Bud to accompany him to the back room in the pool hall. The office was decorated with a variety of mounted animal heads with a large set of elk horns mounted above a desk. Barton waved Bud toward a large chair as he bent down before a safe, spun the dial a few times and cranked it open. He extracted a stack of $100 bills, counted off ten, set the remainder back into the safe, closed the door and spun the dial.

"First time I ever lost a game not getting even one shot," growled Barton.

"Just dumb luck," answered Bud. "First time I ever did that too."

"I do want a chance to win this back," said Barton as he handed the $1,000 to Bud.

"Well, I've got a proposal for you to consider," answered Bud. "That old bastard of a boss of mine is coming in next week to buy cattle."

"So I've heard," said Barton.

"I'll find out which bank he will have the money deposited into and we can make a quick $200,000 by robbing it before he buys the cattle," said Bud.

"No way," said Barton. "Two of my cousins were killed while trying to rob a bank. Took me years to get even with the bastard who killed them."

Bud now was certain he was looking at Bull Pierce's killer.

Finally he said, "If I get the special carrier's information and route he will be traveling, we could hold him up and get the money that way. Find a place with no witnesses. With two of us, we shouldn't have any trouble."

"Sounds okay to me," said Barton. "What's the split?"

"Twenty-five percent for you, the rest for me," advised Bud.

"Not enough," snarled Barton. "Either I get forty percent or no deal."

"How about a third?" responded Bud.

"You heard me, it's forty percent or no go," said Barton.

"Okay, okay," responded Bud. "I know the courier will be coming over from Dallas next Tuesday. I'll pick you up at noon here at the hall and I'll have his route scouted out by then. I'll pick a remote area for us to intercept him," said Bud.

"Sounds good," responded Barton. "I'll see you on Tuesday at noon."

Bud pulled up in front of Barton's pool hall at noon on Tuesday. Barton stepped out of the doorway, opened the car door and eased himself in. Neither man spoke as Bud drove south from Wichita Falls. After twenty miles or so, Bud stated, "He'll be traveling on back roads away from the main road. They think it is safer."

"Who is they?" asked Barton.

"The firm he works for. They specialize in transporting large sums of money or even valuable items," responded Bud.

Shortly, he turned off the main road onto a gravel road and proceeded about a mile to turn right on another gravel road which appeared to run parallel to the main road they had recently traveled. The sides of the road had numerous pecan trees as well as plowed fields and wild plum bushes. After a half mile or so, they came to a point where the road was intersected by a shallow creek. Near the creek was a clear area which appeared ideal for a picnic or family reunion. Bud pulled the car under the shade of a large pecan tree. As he got out of the car, he said, "The courier should be along in twenty to thirty minutes. This will be a good place to intercept him."

Barton opened the car door and eased himself out into the early afternoon sun. He walked in front of the car and leaned back casually against the car fender.

"You've been awfully quiet for someone who will soon have a real bundle of money," said Bud to Barton.

"I've just been thinkin'," said Barton. "About what?" asked Bud.

"About what my wife told me last night. She went over to Butcher Creek yesterday to visit her brother who's in the pen for robbing banks," said Barton.

Bud stiffened and stepped backward.

"Her brother described a lawman who recently came to visit and tried to get him to talk about those robberies and the person who killed that Sheriff. The description he gave her of the lawman sounds a lot like you."

At that, both men jerked their pistols from their shoulder holsters and fired at each other at a distance of approximately fifteen feet. Each weapon fired three times. Barton's grip on his gun relaxed and he slid down the car fender to a sitting position. Bud also slid down the base of the pecan tree. Both men stared at each other. They were both dead within five minutes.

CHAPTER TWENTY-FIVE

Amarillo, Texas   *Spring 1963*

Ken and Billy Don deliberately bumped shoulders as they strolled down the hall in the athletic building. They both wore their prized athletic jackets, each with their name and position embroidered onto the front. The team supporters provided the entire team with new jackets at the end of each season. Best advertising possible, Coach Tuff had reckoned, as he convinced the supporter club to pony up the funds for the program.

The two boys arrived at the door marked Marv Tuffington, Head Football Coach. They entered the office and said "good morning" to the office receptionist.

"Coach Tuff sent word he wanted to see us," said Billy Don with a wide grin as he admired the girl's ample bosom. She blushed as she keyed the intercom button to announce their arrival to the coach.

"Come in, come in," shouted Coach Tuffington. Billy Don and Ken went through to the inner office which was overflowing with all types of football gear and sports publications. There were two chairs set in front of his desk and he waved toward the chairs as he set the file he had been studying on the desk. "Just wanted to speak with both of you before you graduate and go other ways," said the coach. The nameplate on his desk showed "Coach Tuff," as he had been called in all his years at the University. "It has been a sincere privilege to coach you boys and I understand both of you have high GP averages. I believe either of you would make a fine coach and I would be pleased to have either one or both of you join my coaching staff here at the University."

"That's really quite a compliment," said Ken, "but I plan to volunteer into the Army to serve my military obligation and then attend law school to become a lawyer."

"That's certainly a great future plan. Given your athleticism and intelligence, the Army should be pleased to have your service," said Coach Tuff.

"I've been discussing the possibility of securing entry into their Officer Candidate School, and that's looking good," Ken said.

"How about you, Billy Don, any chance of you joining with Ken to go into the Army?"

"Already tried, but they rejected me due to color blindness. So I'm thinking about going into politics. My grandfather was a well-known country preacher and when he preached, people came from miles around to hear him preach. I asked him one time what was it that he did that caused the people to flock to him. He said to me,

'Well, son, first of all, I tell 'em what I'm gonna tell 'em, then I tells 'em what I tells 'em, and then I tells 'em what I told 'em, and that's all it takes.' Sounds to me like that same strategy should also work with politics as long as you keep tellin' 'em what they want to hear," said Billy Don with a big grin.

"You know, Billy Don, I do believe you will be a successful politician," said Coach Tuff.

Ken did secure an appointment to OCS upon joining the Army. He trained and studied hard and graduated at the top of his class. Ken's unit was included in the U.S. force ordered to the La Drang Valley Vietnam operation in November. This resulted in the first major conflict between U.S. forces and the People's Army of Vietnam, North Vietnam (PAVN). This encounter resulted in the largest and most deadly battle yet in the Vietnam conflict over a period of three days and two nights. U.S. casualties were 234 killed in Action (KIA) and more than 400 Wounded in Action (WIA). North Vietnamese forces suffered 634 KIA and an estimated 1,215 WIA. First Lieutenant Ken Adams was one of the U.S.A. WIA. While in the hospital recovering from his wounds, he was told that his mother died in an automobile accident. Shortly after her funeral, his father married his secretary. It seems they had been interested in each other for some time. His younger brother joined the Navy and was assigned duty aboard an East Coast stationed aircraft carrier. He and Ken rarely corresponded after that.

Billy Don looked at the sign on the door, "Re-elect Representative Cole Pearson." He opened the door and stepped into a beehive of activity. Three women manned telephones set up on a temporary table made by placing a wood door on top of two metal file cabinets. At another table, two young men and a young woman were busy stuffing campaign flyers into envelopes and setting them into envelope containers. He could see three full boxes sitting on the floor near the area where they were working. At another temporary desk, two middle-aged ladies were engaged in a lively discussion about scheduling arrangements. The young receptionist asked if she could be of help. Billy Don handed her a manila folder and said, "This contains a copy of my college transcript along with a letter of recommendation from Dean Almont of Mid-Central University and another from Coach Howard Tuffington. I would like to be of help with Representative Pearson's re-election campaign."

"Have you done any campaign work before?" she asked.

"Well, no, I've been involved with college but now that's behind me, and I'd like to help," said Billy Don.

"Wait here a moment," advised the receptionist as she arose from her desk and marched toward the back of the room to bend down and whisper in the ear of a serious-looking woman at the only real desk in the room. She handed Billy Don's folder to the woman and nodded in his direction. Billy Don put on his best smile and nodded to the severe-looking woman now examining the contents of the folder he had presented to the receptionist.

Shortly, the woman spoke to the receptionist and she came back to her desk.

"Come with me," she said to Billy Don as she turned and stepped back toward the lady seated at the desk. "This is Mrs. Stan Turner, Congressman Pearson's campaign manager," she said as she motioned toward the lady who was still studying the documents contained in his folder.

"Pleased to meet you," said Billy Don as he reached out his hand toward the woman who had yet to even look up at him."

"Shut up and sit down," she responded. "We've got a lot of work going on here and we don't have time to waste on some snot-nosed football player with no political campaign experience."

At this, she leaned back in her chair and examined Billy Don's appearance with some degree of interest.

Billy Don for once in his life was unable to respond and simply smiled at the serious yet attractive woman sitting at the desk.

"Did they teach you anything of value at that shit-kicking university you attended?"

"We studied a variety of subjects that were of interest but probably of minimal value in the real world," responded Billy Don.

"That's probably the most honest statement made by the whole bunch of college campaign volunteers we have picked up this term. At least you know you don't know shit about how a campaign operates," said Mrs. Turner. "My name is Mildred but you can call me Mil – that's what everybody else does," she said. "Just to make it clear, the whole reason for a campaign committee is to raise money and keep the candidate from stepping on his dick."

Billy Don's mouth dropped and he said, "I don't believe that was quite how our instructor outlined the function in college."

"Well, that's it in a nutshell and where would you fit into that scenario?" asked Mil.

"I know a lot of wealthy athletic supporters from my career in football at the University," said Billy Don. I'd be good at introducing Congressman Pearson to them and gaining admittance to their functions. I'm sure they could provide substantial contributions and I'm good at reading people and making friends quickly," said Billy Don.

At this, Mil smiled and said, "I believe we can find a place in the campaign for you. Also, as handsome and good-looking as you are, the young female voters should flock to our side as well as some of the middle-aged ladies too. Hell, the old bats will all want to mother you to death, so it looks like you made the grade. I think we may have a long-time association in the making."

CHAPTER TWENTY-SIX

Hendley, Texas   *Spring 1965*

D usk fell onto the house slowly as Kathy May let herself into the back door leading into the kitchen. She placed the small bag of groceries onto the counter and began the process of storing and putting away her supplies. She picked up the postcard from the counter, addressed to her from Ken, and read, *I'll be home on Saturday to see you and you'll know first-hand that I have well-recovered from the wound recently received. Hardly even a limp left to show for it.* She looked at her calendar and crossed off Friday and saw again where she had simply written "Ken" on the block for Saturday. She began the process of preparing her cup of tea and a simple meal of crackers and cheese spread. She soon poured the tea and, taking the plate and saucer, moved slowly into the parlor where the television set was reporting on the details of the battles being fought in Vietnam that day. She set her plate and saucer onto the small side table and slowly sat down into her comfortable chair. She sighed and then thought she heard a noise over her shoulder.

"Who's there?" she asked as she turned slowly to peer into the semi-dark room. Again she asked, "Who's there?" and then with a look of astonishment she gasped and said, "Jackie, is that you? Is that really you?" She blinked and stuttered. She slowly turned sideways and said, "Why, Jackie, you haven't changed at all – you're just the same." She gasped once again, clutched her chest and said, "Is it now – am I coming with you? Please don't go . . ." and slowly crumpled to the floor.

The Jordan Bus crunched on the gravel as it pulled to a stop in front of the bus depot. The driver exited first and bent to retrieve a duffle bag from the lower storage compartment. Ken stepped down from the bus, cane in hand, thanked the driver, picked up his bag and moved toward a waiting taxi. His walk was slow and the limp of his right leg only slightly perceptible. He handed the bag to the cab driver and asked him to take him to 1154 Walnut. The driver said, "Yeah, sure," and got into the driver's seat. Ken opened the back door and slid in. As the cab backed out from the bus depot, the driver asked, "Wounded in Vietnam, huh?"

"Yeah, little more than a scratch," replied Ken with a wry smile.

The driver gave him a condescending look and said under his breath, "Why the hell are we there anyway?" This wasn't the first time Ken had experienced people letting him know they did not approve of the war or of him even being in his uniform.

"We're there because our government made a commitment to be there to help the people of that country."

"Yeah, well, maybe our government made a commitment but the people of this country sure as hell didn't." The rest of the trip was made in silence. Ken knew he would not change the driver's opinion no matter what he said, so it was just as well to let it be. The cab driver asked over his shoulder, "Just what kind of people are those Congs anyway?"

"Do you mean the Viet Cong fighters?" asked Ken.

"Yeah, those Cong guys the TV is always talkin' about."

"Well, they're pretty determined and committed. After all, Vietnam is their country."

"Yeah but they're killing their own countrymen as well as our guys too. I just sure don't understand that war," said the driver.

"You and a whole lot of other people," said Ken.

The cab stopped in front of Kathy May's house and Ken paid the driver and also included a nice tip.

The driver grudgingly said, "Thanks, have a nice day," as he dropped Ken's bag onto the sidewalk.

Ken slowly made his way up the walk, all the time taking in the lawn and pecan trees he had so eagerly harvested the nuts from as a boy. He smiled to himself as he recalled climbing into each tree and causing the nuts to rain down like hail onto the ground. His spirits lightened when he crossed the porch and lifted the old door knocker. Once, twice, three times with no answer. He peered into the windows and called out, "Miss Kathy May, Miss Kathy May, are you home?" With no answer, he slowly made his way around to the side of the house to the back porch. He knocked on the door, tried the knob and swung the door open. As he entered he called again, "Miss Kathy May, are you here?"

He moved slowly through the kitchen into the parlor where he saw her frail body slumped onto the floor next to her chair. The television set played a silly Howdy Doody show with Buffalo Bob moving things along. Ken felt for Kathy May's pulse and finding none, he put his hand to her forehead and began to sigh slowly and softly. Finally, he rose up, turned off the TV and went back to the kitchen.

Ken looked through the stack of mail and papers collected in a small basket on the end of the counter until he found an envelope from her attorney, Clayton Brewster. He picked up the telephone and called. When Clayton answered, Ken told him who he was and that he was at Kathy May's house and what he had found. Clayton was silent for just a moment and then advised he would make all the necessary calls. He asked if Ken would remain until he could get there with the medical examiner. Almost as if in a trance, Ken advised that he would.

Finally, Clayton said, "Ken, you know she loved you very much."

"Yes, and I loved her," Ken said.

When Clayton arrived with the medical examiner and two attendants from the local funeral parlor, he again asked Ken to remain. Clayton directed the examiner and attendants to where Kathy May was lying. While they were examining her, he and Ken sat down at the kitchen table. Clayton started out, "She may have had a premonition about all this. She left very explicit instructions on how she wanted things handled. You know she had no surviving relatives. She left everything to you."

Ken sat shocked, staring at Clayton.

"She was a very wealthy woman with an interesting passion. Her father had successfully drilled a number of oil wells when she was quite young. She always held onto his half interest in them and the income they generated, and wisely invested the funds. She left well over $10 million dollars to you. Her will names you as her sole beneficiary with a codicil that you continue her passion. You see, she believed the reason her father had gained success was due to the Indian's trust in showing him where to drill for oil."

The medical examiner came to stand near the table and said, "It would appear that she was just overcome by a stroke. We'll know more after the autopsy but I did not see any sign of a struggle or foul play."

"Yes," said Clayton, "her health had been declining over the past few years and I believe she knew this was coming."

"I'll be in contact in the next few days to file the Death Certificate," the examiner said as he turned to Ken. "It does not appear that your mother suffered in any way."

Ken said, "Thank you, that is appreciated but she was not my mother. Although she certainly treated me like a son."

The medical examiner followed the attendants out with Kathy May. Ken and Clayton watched as the hearse moved slowly down the street.

Ken said to Clayton, "You mentioned this passion Miss Kathy May had, what was it?"

"She helped support numerous Indian orphanages – seeing that the boys and girls in them received good medical care as well as improved educational opportunities. I believe at last count, she had provided funds to assist in a college education for more than 500 orphans. She was always there to help assist financially and emotionally. After all, she felt that all she had came from the help the Indians provided to her father early on in his career."

"Her will directs that you manage the income from her investments and the continuing royalties from the producing oil wells. She further stipulated that you should receive a stipend of ten percent of the yearly income, not to be less than $75,000 per year. The process of distributing the rest of the annual receipts are all laid out in her will as well. I know she intended to see that you had an opportunity to go on to law school after completing your military service. This way, you can go wherever you desire. After you complete law school, I would be pleased to have you join my law firm. We have a good staff of experienced, capable associates and partners. I believe you will make a great lawyer."

CHAPTER TWENTY-SEVEN

Southern Oklahoma   *Winter 1965*

Ken stood at the entrance to the Indian orphanage and noted the name above the door: Okonakee – Home to All. He stepped through the doorway and moved to the reception desk. "I'm Ken Adams," he announced to the young receptionist, "and I called yesterday to set up a meeting with the Superintendent."

The receptionist announced his arrival with the intercom on her desk. "Mr. Opalla is expecting you, go right in," she said, as she motioned toward the door behind her. As Ken stepped through the door, the Superintendent rose from his desk and stepped around to greet him warmly. "We are so sorry to hear about Miss Kathy May. For as long as I have been here at Okonakee, she has always been a true friend and loyal supporter."

"I only recently learned the degree of her involvement with the sites and wanted to know more about her role here," said Ken.

"Well, as you probably know, we receive some amount of support from the government via the tribal council, but it was Miss Kathy May who filled in the 'extras' – especially to assist our charges in pursuit of extended education efforts. We are fortunate that she has helped numerous young people with scholarships, grants and outright gifts of her fortune. Many of these young people have achieved great success, some have become lawyers, doctors and accountants, and our state legislature has more than one member who benefitted from her support. Many of these now find it in their hearts to give back – not only in her method but also by adopting their sisters and brothers who thereby step from our doors into a greater land of opportunity."

"Miss Kathy May requested that I continue her passion in helping those of your nation in need. What can I do to help continue her involvement?"

"Our nation feels it is important for our people to not lose sight of who we are and where we came from. Our ancestors were here for thousands of years before the white man arrived from Europe. Our ancestry and heritage become dimmer every day as we become more integrated into the modern world, which is inevitable. There are fewer and fewer experiences for us to know the true way of the ancients. To help establish educational programs that portray the ancient way of life is important to our nation. There never seems to be any money to do this as everything goes just to 'make it by.' If we could develop a program to provide a continuing experience on the ways of the ancients, it would be good for our people."

"Obviously, you've spent some time thinking about this – what sort of programs would you propose?" asked Ken.

"I believe our people would benefit from a program providing public attendances and participation in the dances and rituals of the ancients. We could offer such participation to our young people and help regenerate their knowledge and pride in the way of the ancients. Over time, I believe others would benefit from those experiences as well. This would provide a method of keeping the way and beliefs of our nations from dying out."

"I believe you have a great vision for your nation and I believe other nations and tribes would agree. Please proceed with plans to draw up such a program. I'll have Miss Kathy May's attorney get in touch to set up a process to properly fund such a program. Please see that other tribes and nations contact him for assistance as well," said Ken.

Thus was formed the "Rites and Rituals of the Ancients." These groups set up ceremonial celebrations and exhibitions of many of the tribes of North America. Some of these ceremonial celebrations last for two or three days at a time and are accompanied by many members of the tribes. They are a very important part of continuing the heritage of the various tribes.

CHAPTER TWENTY-EIGHT

Amarillo, Texas   *Spring 1973*

Ken smiled when he saw the sign as he drove onto the campus of Mid-Central State University.

"Welcome back, Bull Doggers." The Bull Doggers name had never been officially adopted by the University, but it was dearly loved by the student body, so it stuck. Ken was glad to be attending his ten-year college reunion. He had seen a television interview with State Representative Billy Don Preston announcing that he was planning to attend the reunion, and Ken hoped they might get to meet and bring each other up-to-date on their lives. Ken figured his best chance to meet would be at the all-athletics get-together planned for that evening at the University Athletic Center at 7 o'clock. He checked into his suite at the Ox Tree Hotel, hung up his clothes and grabbed a long shower with plenty of hot water. He remembered his days of youth being raised in the rural Hendley,

Texas, area where water came from a well and was almost always in short supply. His father had yelled at him on many occasions to "Shut that shower off, soap and rinse down quickly." He marveled how so many people had no real appreciation of the convenience of abundant clean water. He selected a pair of gray slacks with a white oxford shirt and a blue blazer, no tie. Dressy enough to be dressy but not over the top. He left his car at the hotel and took a cab to the Athletic Center, and was surprised to see a line of people waiting to enter the facility. He recognized a few of his old teammates and observed they all appeared twenty pounds heavier than when they had played football together. Each sported pretty or beautiful wives, some of whom Ken recognized from his college days.

Eventually, they made their way into the facility, and armed with stick-on name tags, entered the large, open area on the center court. Numerous tables were placed around and each sported a banner advertising a group, fraternity, club or athletic group. About a dozen tables were devoted to football and Ken made his way to one where he recognized fellow teammates.

"Ken, you Dogger you!" yelled one of his linemen while giving him a bear hug and slapping him soundly on the back. "Read about some of your activities in Nam. How's that leg doing? You don't even look like you have a limp!"

"Only on cold rainy days," answered Ken.

As the lineman was introducing his wife, Pam, a loud buzz began at the entrance to the facility, soon followed by a cheer as Billy Don Preston made his way into the crowd.

"How y'all doin' today?" yelled Billy Don as the crowd yelled back, "Just fine Billy Don!"

With his hands held high and signaling for quiet, Billy Don announced, "We've got a special treat today. Will you just take a look at who rode in with me today?" at which he motioned for the recently retired Coach Marv Tuffington to come and join him. The crowd went wild. As Coach Tuff joined him, Billy Don held his hands high in the air like a champion prizefighter. "I do believe this man could be elected Governor if he just said the word," yelled Billy Don.

Again the crowd roared and the chant began, "Nuff for Tuff, Nuff for Tuff, Nuff for Tuff."

Coach Tuff was all smiles as he turned to the crowd to say, "I really had no plans to attend today but Billy Don simply would not take no for an answer. Now if you have not yet been exposed to the persuasiveness of Billy Don, you are in for a treat. The man simply will not take no for an answer and eventually you just give up for him to get his way." The crowd roared.

"Hell it works that way down in Austin, too, where it's known as the Preston Press!" yelled Billy Don. He began moving around the room meetin' and greetin', as the politicians call it. He eventually made his way to Ken's table, grabbed him in a bear hug and said, "It is really great to see you again. I was so concerned you might not make it back from the war. Are you still feeling the zip flow?"

Before Ken even had a chance to reply, Billy Don said, "Looky here now, we're setting up a reception over at the Mooreland Hotel. Gotta meet with some of the good ol' boys and press the flesh after we get out of here. Come on over and meet the staff. We'll have time to laugh about the good old days."

With that Billy Don was on to the next group, all the while keeping a running conversation going with his entourage. Ken laughed and shook his head. Some things just never change.

After visiting with more of his old teammates, Ken eventually was able to excuse himself and called a cab to take him to the Mooreland Hotel, the most elegant and expensive hotel in the area. Upon arrival at the hotel, he saw a sign in the entryway announcing, Preston Party, Main Ballroom. He had no problem locating the room as it seemed half the people in the hotel were heading for the party. As he entered, two staff people asked his name and they directed him to the registration table where a name tag had been prepared for him. Ken estimated there had to be 200 people at the party. Waiters were busy circulating through the crowd with trays of drinks and finger foods of many varieties. Ken accepted a glass of red wine, which he found to be quite good. Billy Don was surrounded by dozens of people, hanging on every word he spoke. Again, Ken laughed and shook his head. An attractive young woman saw his head shake and with a questioning look asked Ken if he knew Billy Don. Ken explained that yes, they had been roommates and teammates for the four years both attended the university.

"Oh, so you're Ken Adams," said the young woman with a smile, as she extended her hand. "My name is Kay Bivens. I'm a speechwriter for Representative Preston, been on staff for four years now." Her handshake was firm and confident. "He talks about your relationship frequently and often says he regards you as a role model for people he tries to recruit for the various posts for which he is responsible."

Ken asked if she would care for something to drink and she said a glass of sparkling water would be great, but even more appreciated would be someplace to just sit down. She stated she had been on her feet all day and her feet were really killing her. Ken directed her to an area near the rear of the hall where he had seen a few dozen tables set up when he first arrived. He located an empty table, held a chair for her and stated he would be back in a minute. He made his way to the service bar, secured two glasses of sparkling water, each with a slice of lime. He returned to the table, set one glass of water before Kay and seated himself across from her.

"Now, tell me, how did you become a speechwriter for Billy Don?" Ken asked.

"After graduating from the university, I was acquainted with Mil Turner, his campaign manager, and she offered me a job on his staff as a speechwriter."

"What was your major in college?" asked Ken.

"Creative writing," advised Kay. "Always planning to write The Great Novel, but also necessary to pay rent and live," said Kay. "The job takes a lot of time and sometimes I just feel wrung out. The Great Novel will just have to wait," she said with a wry smile. "What about you?"

Ken filled her in on his history with details about his relationship with Miss Kathy May Dillard. He said he remained active in his law practice and fitted in the details about administering the estate of Miss Kathy May.

Kay said she thought Miss Kathy May's wish to have her estate continue helping Indian orphanages was great. Ken explained that over the years, a number of the orphanages ceased to function and more of the proceeds of the estate were distributed to a number of tribes who sponsored "Rites and Rituals of the Ancients" to help promulgate the ancient beliefs and celebrations of the tribes.

As the evening progressed, Ken became more infatuated with Kay Bivens. Eventually, most of the people had left and Billy Don and Mil Turner sat down at the table with Ken and Kay.

"Glad to see you two getting acquainted," said Billy Don. "Always thought the two of you would get along well."

"Well, it looks like the evening was a success for you," said Ken to Billy Don.

"More than expected. There's a group pushing for me to run for the Lieutenant Governor slot this fall. And, hell, I just might do it as long as Mil here agrees to stay on and handle the campaign."

"You know I'll stay," said Mil. "We've been successful on the last three, why not make it four?"

"How about you, Kay, you good to stay on?" asked Billy Don.

"Sure, that Great Novel can wait."

Billy Don looked at Ken and asked, "How about you? You doin' anything bigger than helpin' me campaign?"

"Me?" answered Ken. "I'm not into politics but if you ever need a good lawyer, I'm your man."

At that Billy Don was up and on his way across the room to bid farewell to the last guests.

"And that's how he does things," said Mil. "And he'll win too. Probably the country's most natural politician. All ego and B.S., but he wins. That's all that matters," said Mil as she rose from her chair. "Time to call it a night. Tomorrow's another day and God only knows what new opportunities will present themselves." At that, Mil headed to the entry and off to her room.

Ken looked at Kay and asked, "Is it like this all the time?"

"Pretty much so." She extended her hand as she rose from her chair, and said, "I have really enjoyed getting to know you."
Ken said that he had enjoyed meeting her too. "You know, I'd really like to know you better. Would you be available to enjoy a country picnic with me tomorrow afternoon?"

She replied, "That would be very nice. At what time?"

"I'll pick you up at 3 o'clock and we'll be back before dark," said Ken.

"Sounds great, see you at 3."

The next afternoon, Ken's car came to a halt in front of the Mooreland Hotel at precisely 3 o'clock. Kay was waiting in the entryway dressed in a light summer dress and sandals. A large sun hat and sunglasses completed her appearance. Ken was spellbound at her natural beauty. He had dated a number of young women in his life, but never had any type of serious relationship. He escorted her to his car, a new Buick convertible.

"It's a nice day, how about we put the top down and live dangerously?" asked Ken with a laugh.

Kay laughed and said, "Sounds fine to me. It's been years since I rode in a convertible with the top down."

A wooden picnic basket rested on the back seat. "The hotel staff was kind enough to pack a picnic meal suitable for a king. Of course, the nice tip helped in their enthusiasm," said Ken.

As they motored easily through the streets of Amarillo, Ken glanced at Kay frequently. Finally, he could not contain himself and he blurted out, "You really are a beautiful woman."

Kay laughed and said, "My, my what a smooth talker you are, Mr. Adams."

Ken's cheeks reddened at which she laughed again.

"You've never had a real girlfriend have you?" Her tone was light and easy, more an observation than a statement.

"No, not a REAL girlfriend," responded Ken. "How about you, how many REAL boyfriends have you had?"

"Of course, one would need to define what REAL means as it would probably be different for each of us," responded Kay.

"Spoken like a true lawyer," replied Ken. "Did you ever study law while earning your degree?"

"No, but I have read a lot of books written by lawyers."

"Speaking of books, who would you regard as your favorite author?" asked Ken.

"Easy for me to say, my favorite author is John Steinbeck," responded Kay.

"That's really something," said Ken, "Steinbeck is my favorite as well."

They spent the rest of the ride discussing their interpretations of Steinbeck's various works. Ken said his favorite Steinbeck work was *The Grapes of Wrath*. Kay said she was torn between *The Red Pony* and *Tortilla Flat*. They both agreed *Of Mice and Men* was very humanly perceptive. Ken felt Steinbeck's later book *Travels with Charley*, written near the end of his life, revealed more of Steinbeck's sense of humor than his other works.

Soon, they arrived at the picnic place Ken had in mind when inviting Kay the evening before. A smooth area with shade trees near a small lake seemed quite peaceful and pleasant for a Sunday afternoon picnic. He spread a blanket onto the grass, escorted Kay to have a seat while he set the basket at the edge of the blanket. He opened the basket and extracted two bottles of seltzer water from an iced container, opened both and handed one to Kay. They spent the afternoon becoming better acquainted and filling in the details of their lives.

At each passing hour, Ken could feel himself becoming more and more infatuated with this young woman. Near sunset, they observed a flock of ducks descend onto the surface of the lake close to their picnic spot. In the distance from the woods came the call of a whippoorwill and soon nearby an answer from his mate. Ken told Kay the story relayed to him by Miss Kathy May how her parents had heard a pair of calling birds on a pleasant evening stroll as they fell in love. Kay said that was one of the most romantic stories she had ever heard.

"Me too," said Ken, as he took her in his arms and kissed her gently. He said, "I do believe you are the most beautiful girl I have ever known. And I believe I am falling in love with you even after just these past two days. Let's spend time together and see if you develop similar feelings for me."

"I think that is a really good idea," said Kay. "You are the most remarkable man I have ever met. You are correct that we need to give these feelings time to mature and I'm looking forward to that time."

They managed to see each other frequently and their love for each other grew stronger at each encounter. Six months after meeting, Ken asked Kay to marry him and she joyfully responded, "Yes, forever."

They were married six months later with Lieutenant Governor Billy Don Preston as Ken's best man.

Billy Don served two terms as Lieutenant Governor of Texas and entered his name in the next race for Governor. It was a nasty hard-fought election, but he finally was declared the winner. At the Governor's victory reception, Mil Turner asked for a private meeting with the Governor.

"Well, Billy Don, we've come a long way together. But this is the end of the line for me. I've covered up your last shenanigan. You're not being true and faithful to your wife and I can't work for you anymore. I'm tired of buying off or threatening into submission these dim-witted, big-tittied bimbos you keep turning up in bed with. If you could learn to keep your pecker in your pants, there's no telling how far you could go. But it will be without me. I'm through." And with that, Mil Turner marched out the door, head held high and never looked back.

Billy Don smiled as he said to himself, "You know, I'm gonna miss that woman. She had a really big set of balls."

CHAPTER TWENTY-NINE

Washington, D.C.   *Spring 1985*

The television anchor was continuing his presentation: "Today, in Washington, D.C., the President is expected to announce his choice for the replacement of Justice Michael Andrews of the Supreme Court, who passed away last week just days after his eighty-eighth birthday. It is widely anticipated that the President will be nominating someone he has known from a long personal basis, as he has done in selecting most of his cabinet appointments. One report advised his college roommate was seen arriving at the airport this morning and it is doubted to be just a coincidence. The news conference is scheduled for 11 o'clock Eastern Time and we will have our crew there for that conference. Now on to this weekend's baseball schedule."

The aide was calling his name softly and gently touching his shoulder, "Judge Adams, Judge Adams, they're just about ready for you."

Ken blinked and rubbed his eyes, "Sorry, I guess the travel and time change took more out of me than I thought." He grinned at the aide. "I guess it's not every day that someone falls asleep while waiting to see the President."

The aide laughed and said it has happened more than once, but not a lot.

Ken looked back at the desk – nothing had changed – the magnifying glass laid just as it had. Ken smiled to himself, shook his head and said to the aide, "Funny how some seemingly innocuous items can set your memory working overtime."

"I suppose," responded the aide. He followed Ken's gaze to the desk but did not see anything out of place. "Are you sure you're alright?" he asked.

"Oh, yes, of course." Ken stood and began to adjust his tie.

"There's a washroom over there if you'd care to freshen up."

"Thanks, I do believe I could use a little freshening," said Ken. He walked through the doorway to the washroom, ran water in the sink, splashed a little onto his face and eyes, washed a mouthful around his mouth and spit it out while making a face. "You'd think the water at the White House would taste better," said Ken.

"Plumbing improvements are in the budget this year, but then again, they were in the budget last year as well, but got cut at the last minute."

Ken straightened his tie and ran his fingers through his hair while looking in the mirror. "Well, I do believe I've tasted better branch water down on the plains in my previous life. During the summers while in college, I used to do a little cowboying – branch water coffee is definitely an acquired taste," Ken gave the aide a smile. "Not that I would recommend it today."

The door to the study opened and in walked President William Donald Preston with a half dozen followers – each busily scribbling the instructions he was issuing non-stop. "And be sure Senator Carleton and his wife are on the invitation list – we need his vote to get the Farm Bill through – and he knows it. Put them at the table with the Vice President so he can work on him." He turned to Ken with the great smile that had helped him charm his way through life – Billy Don Preston had handled his political career with the same confidence and style he had employed while charming the football crowds at Mid-Central State University.

"Ken, I want to thank you for agreeing to help me out, you always said to call on you if I needed a good lawyer and I believe this qualifies. I've followed your career and been greatly impressed with your accomplishments. I hope you won't mind if I share a few of those with the press during our announcement."

It was all said in such a genuine way that it would have been impossible to not agree. Ken could see how the stories he had heard could be true – the President had such a presence that it would be difficult to not agree with him. "Of course, Mr. President. But I do need to have you understand that I make my own decisions."

"Well, hell, I know that, wouldn't want it to be any other way – I'd put my trust in your decisions any day."

The aide announced, "They're ready for you, Mr. President."

"Well, let's not keep them waiting," said the President.

The television commentator was droning on, "As has been the case throughout President Preston's term, he has recruited from his circle of friends and associates to fill key positions in his administration. Judge Ken Adams is the latest to receive the President's request to fill a key position – the camera swung back onto the President and Ken as they stepped toward the podium in the press room.

"Thank you all for coming today. I have the distinct pleasure to introduce you to one of the finest Americans you could ever know. Ken Adams and I attended college together and even played football on the same team. Of course, that was in the days before the 240-pound linebackers who can also run like gazelles."

At this the crowd gave a murmured laugh and the President responded with that special smile – the one that made you think he had just shared something private and special with each person in the room. "Judge Adams spent time serving his country in Vietnam and although he would never share it with you, he was twice decorated for heroic acts. After his discharge from the service, he attended law school at Harvard and then returned to pass the bar exam in Texas and ultimately became one of the most respected trial judges in the nation. His rulings and opinions were always clear and concise and supported the rule of law as the basis for consideration. He will make a truly great Supreme Court Justice."

As the President spoke, Ken's gaze wandered past him to the door open to the study where he had waited. He could see the desk and the magnifying glass laying on top. He thought again of the time many years ago when Mr. Peltier had startled his concentration on the magnifying glass, which even now rested on his desk at home.

AFTERWORD

North Central Texas, *Present Day*
Southern Oklahoma

S hould you be fortunate enough to find yourself strolling slowly down a remote country lane on a spring or early summer evening, the chances are pretty good you will hear the lonesome call of a whippoorwill. It will help if the country lane is flanked with wild blossoming plum bushes. The air is scented with a sweet perfume. Should you be even more fortunate to be enjoying such a stroll with a beautiful and charming young woman, the chances are very good that you will either be in love or will be falling in love. As you hear the distant response to that lonesome call, whip-poor-will, whip-poor-will, I guarantee you will come to a halt, hold your precious one close and listen as the two lonesome calls come ever closer and closer. I really can't think of a more romantic experience and I guarantee you will hope that moment could last forever.

All of the characters in *The Calling Birds* are fictional, as are most of the locations, although Amarillo, Texas, is a thriving major city. In the process of writing this story, I frequently wondered if anyone would actually believe that a white lady spinster who had inherited a fortune would spend her life giving it away to help support Indian orphanages. It would require a stretch to believe. In the process of researching information on Indian orphanages, I read a book written by Marilyn Irvin Holt which was published in 2001. There were two sentences on Page 239 of her book where Mrs. Holt mentioned "$40,000 had been contributed to construct a school for young Indians on White Clay Creek located on the Pine Ridge Reservation in Dakota Territory. The donation was from Katharine Drexel and the school opened in March of 1890."

I then looked for information on Katharine M. Drexel, and from the internet learned the following:

Born: November 26, 1858, Philadelphia, Pennsylvania

Died: March 3, 1955, Bensalem, Pennsylvania

Father: Francis Anthony Drexel, Died 1885

Mother: Hannah Langstroth, Died January 1859

Katharine M. Drexel's family was wealthy. They had traveled to the Western states in 1884 where she saw the plight and destitution of Native Americans. She wanted to do something specific to help. Thus began her lifelong personal and financial support of numerous missions and missionaries in the United States.

Katharine and her two sisters were still mourning their father's death when they sailed to Europe in 1886. Their father left behind a $15.5 million estate of which approximately $1.5 million was distributed to various charities. The remaining $14 million was held in trust with only the income from the trust to be distributed to Katharine and her sisters.

The sisters shared the income produced by the inheritance, about $1,000 per day for each woman. In current dollars, the estate would be worth about $400 million.

In January 1887, the sisters were received in a private audience by Pope Leo XIII. Katharine requested the church to send missionaries to help the Indians. To their surprise, the Pope suggested that Katharine become a missionary. Drexel decided to give herself to God, along with her inheritance, through service to American Indians and Afro-Americans.

In May of 1889, Drexel entered the Sisters of Mercy convent in Pittsburgh to begin her six-month postulancy.

On February 12, 1891, Drexel professed her first vows as a religious, dedicating herself to work among American Indians and Afro-Americans in the Western and Southwestern United States. She helped establish a religious congregation, the Sisters of the Blessed Sacrament. She and her sister nuns opened a boarding school, St. Katharine's Indian School in Santa Fe, New Mexico. A few years later, she helped finance the work of the friars among the Pueblo Native Americans in New Mexico. In all, Drexel established fifty missions for Native Americans in sixteen states.

When Mother Katharine purchased an abandoned university building to open Xavier Preparatory School in New Orleans, vandals smashed every window. Nonetheless, Drexel made possibly her most famous foundation in 1915, Xavier University,

New Orleans, the first such institution for black people in the United States.

Mother Katharine died at the age of ninety-six. Because neither of her biological sisters had children, after her death, pursuant to their father's will, the Sisters of the Blessed Sacrament no longer had the Drexel fortune available to support their ministries. Nonetheless, the order continues to pursue its original apostolate, working with Afro-Americans and Native Americans in twenty-one states and Haiti.

Her cause for beatification was introduced in 1966. Pope John Paul II formally declared Drexel "Venerable" on January 26, 1987. Mother Drexel was canonized on October 1, 2000. Numerous parishes and schools bear the name of St. Katharine Drexel.

There are a number of interesting similarities between St. Katharine Drexel and a lead character in my book, Miss Kathy May Dillard. First of all, both Katharine Drexel and Kathy May Dillard shared similar names. Both their initials were K.M.D. and Kathy is a shortened version of Katharine. Neither ever married and both their fathers left sizeable fortunes to their daughters, the proceeds of which they used to benefit American Indians, and in the case of Sister Katharine, Afro-Americans as well.

My fictional character Miss Kathy May had one brother and Sister Katharine had two sisters, none of them ever married. Miss Kathy May's fictional address was 1154 Walnut Street in Hendley, Texas, and Sister Katharine Drexel's family home address was 1503 Walnut Street in Philadelphia. During her lifetime, Katharine Drexel spent about $20 million of her private fortune building schools and churches as well as paying the salaries of teachers in rural schools for blacks and American Indians.

Upon their deaths, St. Katharine Drexel and Miss Kathy May Dillard had no living heirs and their fortunes were left to non-relatives. In the case of St. Katharine, the balance of her father's fortune was awarded to a series of charities as designated in her father's will. Miss Kathy May's fictional fortune was left to be administered by Ken Adams, the young man she loved like a son, with directions to continue helping American Indian orphanages and various tribal activities to help keep memories of the "Ways of the Ancients" from dying out.

The Calling Birds had been completely written before I learned of the life of St. Katharine Drexel.

James R. Barrett

ABOUT THE AUTHOR

I was raised in the '40s and '50s in southern rural Oklahoma. We had no electricity or running water, so our water supply came from a 50-foot-deep well, using a rope and a bucket. Most of our food we raised ourselves, such as hogs, cattle and chicken. If we didn't raise it, we hunted it. My dad could knock a squirrel out of a tree at twenty yards with a slingshot. A half-acre vegetable garden filled the table with ripe tomatoes, onions, okra, beans and a good supply of potatoes.

Birthday and Christmas presents could always be counted on to be socks, shirts or underwear. I learned very early that if there was something I wanted, it was up to me to earn the money to buy it. Thus, I bought my first car when I was just fourteen, with $350 I earned by mowing lawns, hoeing gardens, or harvesting pecans from my father's orchard. My first real job was at fifteen, where I helped clear a warehouse that had burned down. I suppose they liked my work ethic, as they asked me to continue after the new warehouse was built. I started my first company when I was thirty years old. Along the way, my wife and I employed as many as sixty-five employees at a time. Our last company sold in 2010 with retirement soon after.

This is Jim Barrett's first novel. Over the years, clips and snippets came to him until after retirement, he finally had time to organize and arrange the parts into order. Although he spent his life as an engineer, he always enjoyed reading a wide range of topics from science fiction to non-fiction history.

A few of the characters in *The Calling Birds* blossomed from people known in his youth with others completely fabricated. They present a broad spectrum of characters whose lives intertwine and overlap in ways that bring out their activities and loves in unique ways.

Now retired in Southern California, he loves spending time with his grandchildren with frequent fishing trips, travel and getting together with old friends and classmates. He is well into his second novel, *Confessions of a Teenage Bootlegger*, and looks forward to its upcoming publication.

Jim is available to address your literary group, book clubs or just a nice cup of coffee to recount old times and experiences. Contact him via email at marinpub10@gmail.com.